Chaos in Death
and
Possession in Death

J. D. Robb

ISIS

LARGE
PRINT

First published in Great Britain 2013
by
Piatkus
an imprint of
Little, Brown Book Group

First Isis Edition
published 2015
by arrangement with
Little, Brown Book Group
An Hachette UK Company

A catalogue record for this book is available
from the British Library.

ISBN 978–1–78541–099–4 (hb)
ISBN 978–1–78541–105–2 (pb)

Published by
F. A. Thorpe (Publishing)
Anstey, Leicestershire

Set by Words & Graphics Ltd.
Anstey, Leicestershire
Printed and bound in Great Britain by
T. J. International Ltd., Padstow, Cornwall

This book is printed on acid-free paper

CHAOS IN DEATH
AND POSSESSION IN DEATH

In *Chaos in Death*, when eye-witness testimony paints the killer as a green-skinned monster with swollen red eyes and goblin ears, even Eve Dallas is shaken. But as she gets closer, the trail suggests something far more disturbing — someone is playing with science . . . While in *Possession in Death*, after a Gypsy woman whispers her dying words to Eve Dallas, strange things begin to happen. Unable to concentrate on anything, Eve realises that in order to reclaim her mind, she must find the woman's great-granddaughter — one of a string of young missing girls forgotten, or ignored, by all.

CHAOS
IN DEATH

Who knows what evil lurks in the hearts
of men?

> THE SHADOW

Good and evil we know in the field of
this world grow up together almost
inseparably.

> JOHN MILTON

CHAPTER
ONE

He found life in death. And delight in the whirlwind of fear and fright. To hunt, to steal the light, the life, the blood, the soul. Well, he'd been born for it.

It made him laugh to dance around the madness of his creating, cape swirling — and wasn't *that* a wonderful touch — legs kicking in a joyful jig.

Even the sound of his own laughter, deep and rich and free, thrilled him, made him laugh all the harder.

He was *alive*.

"And you're not!"

He hopped, skipped, leaped over the three bodies he'd arranged on the floor. Tilting his head, he grinned at his handiwork. He'd laid them out so they sat — well, slumped, but that was dead for you — in a line against the wall.

Pitiful specimens, really, this trio of junkies who'd barely had the wit or the will to put up a fight. But God knew a man had to start somewhere. Still, their fear was his now, and their tears, their cries and pleas — all his.

It tasted so delicious.

He needed more, of course, so many more. But he'd made a most excellent start. No more playing by the rules, no *sir*! No more Mr. Good Guy.

Boring guy.

He patted his own chest. "I feel like a whole new man."

Chuckling, he stowed the bloody scalpel, the vials, all the lovely specimens in his kit. And inspiration struck.

Clichéd? he asked himself, his head tipping from side to side, his gleaming red eyes bulging with glee and madness as he scanned the room, the bodies, the walls. Maybe, maybe, but irresistible!

After dipping a gloved finger into a pool of congealing blood, he composed his message on the dingy wall. He had to dip back into the well — ha-ha-ha — several times, but the time was well worth it.

To whom it may concern:

Please take out the trash. Don't forget to recycle properly!

Oh, his belly hurt from laughing. He pressed a hand to it, nearly snagging one of the long, pointed nails that stabbed through the glove. Then found himself hesitating before signing his name. He knew his name. Of course, of course he did. For a moment his glee teetered toward fury, his laughter toward guttural grunts.

Then all righted again. He did another quick jig, dipped his finger again.

Thank you for your attention to this matter.

Dr. Chaos.

Perfect. Absently, he sucked the blood and grime from his finger and read the message over twice.

Time to go, he decided. Things to do. And he was absolutely *famished*.

He picked up his kit, lifted an arm in salute.

"Adieu, mes amis!"

On a last cackle of laughter, he turned, swirling the cape — he just loved doing that — as he skipped to the back room and climbed out the window.

He couldn't remember ever having more fun.

And couldn't wait to do it all again.

Lieutenant Eve Dallas studied the scene. Cops saw it all, but there was always something new, some fresh brutality even in the dying summer of 2060 to stretch the boundaries of *all*.

The room stank of blood — so much blood — and death, of fresh puke and piss. Blood soaked into one of the board-thin mattresses shoved into a corner. One of the three victims had died there, she thought. The middle one, she concluded, the black male, age as yet undetermined, with multiple stab wounds and a missing left ear.

Beside Eve, her partner breathed slowly in and out through her teeth.

"If you're going to hurl, Peabody, do it outside."

"I'm not going to hurl." But it came out as a plea rather than a statement.

Eve shifted her gaze, studied Peabody. The short, jaunty, flippy tail she'd pulled her dark hair into looked distinctly out of place now that her skin held a faint green cast. Peabody's dark eyes, slightly unfocused, held their line of sight a few inches above the bodies.

"I just need a minute for everything to settle."

"What was this place?" Eve asked.

"It used to be retail space." Peabody still held her PPC, and her hand was steady enough. "Apartments above, three levels. Slated for rehab." Peabody shut her eyes for a moment.

"Find out who owns it, how long it's been shut down. Take it outside. We need the data," Eve said before Peabody could object. "Get the data."

With a nod, Peabody slipped out the door to where the uniforms responding to the nine-one-one had cordoned off the sidewalk.

With her hands and feet already sealed, her recorder engaged, Eve stepped around and over the debris of shattered bottles, scattered clothes, trash, a broken chair to the bodies.

Her golden brown eyes weren't unfocused, but cop flat. "Three victims, two male, one female, carefully arranged to sit, backs against the front wall. Black male, center, multiple stab wounds, torso, shoulders, arms, legs, neck, and face. Left ear removed. Caucasian female on the left appears to have been strangled. Mixed-race male, right of center, bludgeoned. Left eye removed."

Hell of a party, she thought, and let out a breath that fluttered the bangs on her short cap of brown hair.

"Three mattresses, some bedding, clothes, mini friggie, battery lamp, two chairs, two tables. It appears all three vics flopped here. Money scattered around,

8

what shows looks to be about a grand. So robbery's out. First on scene ascertained forced window, rear of building, street level. Probable point of entry."

She took the female first, hunkered down on her long legs, opened her field kit. "Female also suffered blows to the face, knees. Hard blow to the knees," she murmured. "Pipe, bat, board — take her down — a couple punches. Manual strangulation."

She ran the victim's prints.

"Female is identified as Jennifer Darnell, age twenty-four. Current address listed on West Sixteenth. Got a sheet, including juvie. Primarily illegals busts."

Peabody came back in. "The Whitwood Group bought the property about seven months ago," she said. "From what I can tell, the building was condemned a little over a year ago. Permits for rehab pending."

"Okay. So the killer or killers took his ear, his eye. Isn't there a saying — what is it? Hear no evil, see no evil . . ." Carefully, Eve opened Jennifer Darnell's mouth. "Yeah, speak no evil. He cut out her tongue."

"Jesus."

"Work see-no guy, Peabody. I need ID, TOD." Eve fit on microgoggles, engaged their light to peer into the victim's mouth. "Clean cut, neat and tidy. She was either already dead or unconscious when he took her tongue, and he had a good, steady hand."

Struggling to find her own good, steady hand, Peabody opened her kit. "Taking the body parts, those particular body parts, do you think ritual?"

"Possibly." She looked up at the message on the wall. "Mostly, I think he likes to joke. Real funny guy. He did

9

what he wanted, took what he wanted, now he's telling us to clean up the mess. Dr. Chaos."

Eve looked around the room. "That's what this is. The middle guy? The killer took him out where he lay. Uses a knife, or a scalpel. But he doesn't use it on the others, except for the removal. He switches to bludgeoning for the other male."

"Coby Vix, age twenty-six," Peabody told her. "There had to be two killers, maybe three. One for each vic?"

"Maybe. It's a lot of work for one man. But only one takes credit?"

As Eve had, Peabody studied the bloody message. "Dr. Chaos. It could be the name of a group."

Eve considered it while she used the gauges. "Yeah, it could. TOD on Darnell, two hundred thirty-eight."

"If there was only one, why didn't she run like hell when he's stabbing the bejesus out of that guy or beating the crap out of Vix?"

"Took her out, blows to the knees. Shattered kneecaps. But yeah, it could be more than one. Three distinct methods of killing."

"Vix, TOD two hundred twenty."

"So, he took some time with Darnell. Enough for rape." Eve lifted the hem of the short nightshirt. "No bruising, bleeding, tearing I can see, but the ME will determine sexual assault." Eve lifted the cheap, thin chain around Darnell's bruised neck. "She's wearing a ninety-day chip from Get Straight."

"Vix has sixty." Peabody held up the chip.

With a nod, Eve rose and moved to the middle victim. "Hear-no has thirty. Wilson Bickford," she said when she'd run his prints. "Age twenty-two. That same precision, surgical removal on the ear. Dr. Chaos may just be a doctor, or at least have medical training. Hmm, TOD two hundred thirty. Didn't die first."

She sat back on her heels, tried to see it.

"He's the biggest of the three. The killer went at him first," she continued. "I bet your ass he did."

"Hey, bet your own ass."

"Defensive wounds, hands, arms. Bickford put up a fight. Take it a couple ways. Say three killers, one for each vic. Teamwork. One stabs, one beats, one strangles. But this doesn't look like teamwork," Eve said, scanning the room again. "It looks like . . ." She gestured to the message on the wall.

"Chaos."

"Yeah. Could be the team just went to town on the place. But I'm only seeing one type of bloody footprint, and it's too much to swallow they all wore the same size and type of shoe."

"Missed that," Peabody muttered.

"Maybe there's more, and I've missed them. Or maybe the others were more careful."

"But you don't think so."

"I think that's an interesting gap of time between TODs. I think the same hand did the removals, an experienced hand, steady. We've got serious overkill on the two males, and manual strangulation — which is personal and intimate — on the female. The destruction of the scene is over the top, and that reads rage. But the message is jokey, which reads control and intellect. It could be more than one. One with a cool head, one just batshit crazy.

"Let's get them bagged, tagged, and transported. I want to talk to the nine-one-one caller."

Katrina Chu hunched in the back of the black-and-white, her face white as death, her eyes puffy from weeping. One of the uniforms had gotten her some water. Her throat clicked on every swallow. But to Eve's relief, it looked like Katrina had cried herself out. Her puffy, pale green eyes stayed dry and focused on Eve.

"I need you to tell me what happened," Eve began.

"Jen didn't show up for work. She volunteers on the breakfast shift at Get Straight. The one off Canal. And she and Coby and Wil, they go to the meeting after."

"You worked with her?"

"I'm her sponsor. I work at the free clinic on Canal."

"Louise Dimatto's clinic?"

"Yes. Do you know Dr. Dimatto?"

"Yeah."

The connection seemed to steady her. "I'm an aide there. I'm studying to be a nurse. Jen came into Get Straight a couple months ago, and I offered to be her sponsor. We hit it off. She was really working it, you know? Really trying hard. She got Coby to come in. They wanted to turn their lives around."

"I have her living on West Sixteenth."

"They couldn't pay the rent. They started squatting here a couple weeks ago. Maybe three, I guess. Nobody was using the place, and she said Dr. Rosenthall said it would be okay, for a few weeks."

12

"Dr. Rosenthall?"

"He and Dr. Dimatto donate time to Get Straight. He and Arianna basically fund the organization."

"Arianna."

"Whitwood. They're engaged. Arianna and Dr. Rosenthall. She's a therapist. She donates her time, too. Jen, she wanted to get clean, stay clean. She never missed the morning meeting. And she started working at Slice — a pizza joint — about two months ago. She'd help serve breakfast, take in the meeting, then study for an hour or two — Arianna hooked her up with an online business course — then go to Slice if she had the lunch shift, go into the Center — the Whitwood Center — if she had the dinner shift. But she didn't show up, not to serve breakfast, not for the meeting. She didn't answer her 'link. Neither did Coby or Wil. I got worried."

A tear leaked through after all. "I thought maybe they'd taken a slide. It happens. I didn't want to think it. I really trusted she'd tag me if she got in a situation. But I did think it, so I came by on my way to work, to check on her. I knocked. I couldn't see in the window. It's boarded and grilled, but Jen gave me a key, so I opened it and . . . I saw."

"Do you know anybody who'd want to hurt her, or Coby or Wil?"

"No." Pressing her lips together, she shook her head. "I know some people think once a junkie, but they were trying. They were clean, and trying to stay that way."

"What about people they associated with when they were using?"

13

"I don't know. Jen never told me about any trouble, not this kind. She was happy. I went by Slice last night for takeout, and we talked awhile. She was happy. Coby got a job there delivering, and Wil was working as a stock boy at the twenty-four/seven a couple blocks away. They were going to pool their money and rent a place. Last night she told me they had nearly two thousand in the rent kitty so they were going to start to look for one.

"She was happy."

CHAPTER
TWO

"Run Rosenthall and Whitwood," Eve told Peabody. "And get what you can on the Canal Street Get Straight."

"Already on it. And the sweepers are on their way."

"Good." Eve walked back into the building. "It's going to take them a while to sort through this mess." She poked through a bit. "Credits, cash, even loose change. I'm not finding any 'links."

"They probably had them — who doesn't? — so the killer probably took them."

"Takes the 'links but leaves the scratch. He, or they, didn't care about the money. Just the kill. And if he took the 'links, he either had contact with them or thought they talked about him to each other, or someone else, via 'link."

"It's sad," Peabody murmured. "They were young, and trying to reboot their lives. They had a good chance of making it, too. The floor's clean."

"Suddenly I question your cleanliness standards."

"I mean if you overlook the blood and the mess. It's not dusty or dirty. They kept the floor clean. And see, somebody repaired and painted this chair. They weren't very good at it," Peabody added as she picked up one of the broken legs. "But they tried. And when I checked out the bathroom, I guess it's an employee's restroom deal. Anyway, it was clean. The killers must not have used it. But the vics, they kept it clean."

"Lieutenant?" One of the uniforms stepped in. "We found this in the recycler out back."

He held up the clear protective coat, covered with blood, like the ones she'd seen countless doctors wearing. "Just one?"

"So far, sir."

"Keep checking. Anything pop from the canvass?"

"Not yet."

"Keep on that, too. Bag that for the sweepers. They're on their way. Rosenthall, Peabody."

"Dr. Justin Rosenthall, thirty-eight. He specializes in chemical addictions — and was given a grant by the Whitwood Group for same — cause, rehabilitation. He works primarily out of the Whitwood Center, a facility for the study of addiction, with a health center and visitor's lodging attached. No criminal."

"Let's go see if the doctor's in."

"He's very studly," Peabody added and continued to work her handheld as they walked to the car. "Has numerous awards for service and innovations in his field. Donates time to the Canal Street Clinic, Get Straight, and others."

Peabody slid into the car as Eve took the wheel. "I got lots of pops on gossip and society pages. He and Arianna are quite the item. She's a looker. And really, really rich. Not Roarke rich," Peabody said, referring to Eve's husband, "but she's up there. Or the Whitwood

16

Group — headed by her parents — is. She's thirty-four, a therapist, again specializing in addictions. From the fluff pieces I'm skimming, it looks like they met four years ago, and were engaged last fall. The wedding's set for next month, billed as the wedding of the year. And . . . oh, she had a brother. Chase, died at the age of nineteen. OD'd. She was sixteen. The Whitwood Center opened three years later.

"Oh, listen to this. Rosenthall had a sister. She made it to twenty-two before she OD'd. He was on track to becoming a topflight cardiac surgeon. Switched his focus after his sister's death."

"A surgeon. Gave that up," Eve commented, "to work with junkies. Like his sister, like his fiancée's brother. Day in and day out, seeing them, listening to them, treating them, hearing bullshit out of them. Something could snap."

"Cynic alert. Honest, Dallas, from what I'm reading here, the guy sounds like a saint. A studly saint. Saint Studly of Rosenthall."

"Do you know why the saints are all dead?"

"Why?"

"Because dead's the only way you can pull it off. Living's messy, and everyone living has some dirty little secret. That's why we have jobs."

"A dirty little secret that has a renowned and studly doctor slaughtering three recovering addicts?"

"Somebody did it. He's got the connection, he's got the skill, and according to our source, he's the one who gave them the green light to squat there. If he's so saintly, why didn't he float them a couple months' rent?"

"That's a good question."

"It's one I'm going to ask him."

Old, time-faded brick housed the Whitwood Center. No flash, Eve noted, no gloss — at least not on the exterior — so the building sat comfortably in the old Meatpacking District.

With Peabody, she walked in the front entrance. The lobby area was large and quietly furnished. Comfortable chairs, simple art, some plants gave off the atmosphere of a living area rather than a waiting one despite the reception counter manned by two people.

The man, early thirties, continued to work on his comp while the woman, a few years younger with a pretty face and earnestly welcoming eyes, smiled in their direction.

"Good morning. How can we help you today?"

Eve approached the counter, laid her badge on it. "We need to speak with Dr. Rosenthall."

"I see." The woman didn't so much as blink at the badge. "Is the doctor expecting you?"

"I couldn't say."

"His offices are on the second floor, east. One of his interns or his assistant should be able to help you."

"Okay."

"Stairs to the left, elevators to the right."

As Eve angled left, the woman continued. "You'll want to take the right corridor, go over the garden breezeway, then take the first turn to the left."

18

"Thanks."

"It's nice work," Peabody said as they started up. "The work they've done on the old building. Kept its character. It's comfortable, and it doesn't shout, 'We're really rich philanthropists.'"

On the second floor they walked by several doors, all discreetly shut, with their purposes or a doctor's name on a plaque.

They passed people in lab coats, in street wear, in sharp suits, and in tattered pants. Eve noted the security cameras, and the card slots and palm plates on some of the doors. They passed a nurse's station and the waiting area across from it.

Then they came to the garden breezeway. Below, through treated glass, a central fountain gurgled in a fantasy of flowering plants, shrubs, trees in riotous bloom. White stone benches offered seating, bricked paths wound in an invitation to stroll.

"That says, 'We're really rich philanthropists,'" Eve commented.

"But in a really pretty way."

They made the left into a small blue and cream reception area. The woman behind the counter tapped her earpiece, turned away from the smart screen where, it looked to Eve, she'd been working on updating a complex schedule.

"Can I help you?"

"Lieutenant Dallas and Detective Peabody." Eve held up her badge. "We need to speak with Dr. Rosenthall."

"Is there a problem?"

"There almost always is."

The woman didn't look pleased by the answer, and reminded Eve of Dr. Mira's admin. The dragon at the gates of the NYPSD's shrink and top profiler.

"Dr. Rosenthall's in his lab this morning."

"Where's his lab?"

"I really must insist you tell me your business before I disturb the doctor."

"I really must insist you take us to his lab." Eve tapped her badge. "And this has a lot more insistence than you because it can arrest you for interfering with a police investigation."

"I'll check with the doctor." The words sounded as sour as the woman's face looked. She tapped her earpiece again. "Yes, Pach, would you tell Dr. Rosenthall two police officers are here and insist on speaking with him. Yes. No, they won't say. Thank you." She waited a moment, staring holes through Eve. Then scowled. "Very well."

After another tap, she spoke to Eve. "The doctor's lab assistant will come out and take you back. The doctor will see you."

She aimed her nose in the air before turning back to her screen.

Moments later a side door opened. The man who came out had deep brown skin and large, heavy-lidded eyes nearly as black as his crown of curly hair. He wore a standard white lab coat over jeans and a red T-shirt that asked, "My petri dish or yours?"

"Officers?"

"Lieutenant Dallas and Detective Peabody."

"Oh. Um . . ." He flashed a very white smile. "If you'll come this way?"

Through the door was a maze, a rabbit warren of rooms off angled corridors. The lab assistant negotiated them on flapping gel sandals. He paused at double steel doors, swiped his card, spoke his name. "Pachai Gupta."

The security blinked green in acceptance, and the doors slid open into a large lab. Eve felt a weird juxtaposition as her friend Mavis's voice wailed out about love on the wild side over the pristine red and white room. Strange equations and symbols held frozen on one of the wall screens while something bubbled blue in a heated beaker. A woman with short, sleek red hair hunched over a microscope while her foot tapped to Mavis's grinding beat. Another lab coat diligently worked two comps at a long white counter. He sported a short stub of a ponytail and ragged skids.

In the center of it, amid the coils of tubing, the sparkling electronics, the busy screens, and the forest of test tubes, beakers, and specimen dishes, stood Justin Rosenthall.

He wore a lab coat like other men wore a tux, perfectly fitted and somehow elegant. His gilded mane of hair gleamed under the bright lights. Vid-star handsome, poetically pale, he removed a beaker from its heater with tongs and set it in a bath of water. Steam hissed and curled.

Through the thin curtain of it, Eve saw his eyes, tawny as a lion's, fix intently on some sort of gauge.

"What's he working on?" she asked their guide.

"An antidote."

"To what?"

"To evil." At her raised eyebrows, Pachai flushed, shrugged.

Eve heard a low beep. Justin lifted the beaker again, slid it into a container, sealed it, set another gauge.

Only then did he step back, look over.

"Sorry." There was an absent charm in his smile, in his movements as he crossed to them. "The timing's crucial. You're the police?"

"Lieutenant Dallas, Detective Peabody, NYPSD."

"Dallas. Of course, you're Roarke's wife." His smile warmed as he extended a hand. "It's nice to finally meet you. How is Roarke? I haven't seen him in . . . it's probably been a year. More."

"He's good. This isn't a social call, Dr. Rosenthall."

"Justin. No, of course not. Sorry. How can I help you?"

"You know Jennifer Darnell, Coby Vix, Wilson Bickford."

"Yes." His smile faded. "Are they in trouble? I can assure you they've been working very hard against their addictions. It's a hard road, and there will be stumbles, but —"

"They were murdered early this morning."

Behind her, Pachai let out a strangled gasp as Justin just stared at her. "What? Sorry, what?"

"They were murdered between two and two-forty this morning in the building where they were squatting."

"Dead? Murdered? *All?*"

22

"How?" Pachai took Eve's arm, then quickly released it. His eyes were liquid onyx swimming under inky lashes. They only shimmered more intensely when Justin laid a hand on his shoulder.

"Pach, let's sit down."

"No. No. I'm sorry, but how can they be murdered? I saw them only yesterday."

"When?"

"Pach," Justin repeated, gently. "Music off," he ordered. The redhead called out a protest when Mavis stopped wailing.

"Not now, Marti." Justin rubbed his temple. "There's no mistake?"

"No. When did you see them last?" she asked Pachai.

His lips trembled, and tears continued to swarm those heavy-lidded eyes. "Before Jen and Coby went to work, after Wil got off. We had coffee. We have coffee almost every day."

"You were friends?"

"Yes. We — I — I don't understand."

"No, neither do I," Justin said. "What happened?"

The lab rat with the stubby ponytail had turned and, like the redhead, watched.

"Early this morning Wilson Bickford was stabbed to death, Coby Vix was bludgeoned to death, and Jennifer Darnell was strangled."

Pachai began to weep, and the harsh sobs bore him down to the floor, where he covered his face with his hands.

Justin turned ashen. At her station the redhead sat very still, staring at Eve as if she'd spoken in an ancient

23

foreign language. The other man slumped back in his chair, shuddered, then closed his eyes, lowered his head.

No one spoke.

CHAPTER
THREE

In the silence, Eve gave Peabody a signal, and responding, Peabody moved to Pachai. "I'm sorry for your loss," she began in the comfort voice she used so well. "Let me help you. Let me help you up. Why don't we go over here, sit down?"

"How could — was it — I'm sorry," Justin said. "I just can't think. They were attacked? In the building on West Twelfth?"

"Yes."

"But why, for God's sake? None of them belonged to a gang, none of them had any valuables to speak of. Were these just some random killings?"

"Do you know anyone who'd wish them — any one of them — harm?"

"No. No, I don't. They were turning their lives around, and the three of them had formed a strong bond. Their own small support group."

"They were addicts."

"In recovery," Justin said quickly.

"Was there anyone who they — again any one of them — used to associate with prior to their recovery who might have resented the fact that they were getting clean, staying clean?"

"I don't know, but if so, they didn't mention it to me. If there was someone, something, one of them might have told Arianna. Arianna Whitwood. She was the therapist of record for all three of them."

"Your fiancée."

"Yes." He looked away, pressed his fingers to his eyes. "My God, they were so young, so hopeful."

"You gave them permission to squat in that property."

"Yes. They couldn't make the rent on Jen's apartment. She'd fallen behind before she'd made the commitment to recovery. Pachai told me they were sleeping on the street. I thought . . . it would be a roof over their heads until they found a place."

"You formed an attachment to them?"

"To Jen, then through her to Coby and Wil. She was so determined, and you could see the light coming back into her. You could see her finding her quiet. It was gratifying. Even inspiring."

"I guess I'm curious why you didn't float them the rent."

"I wish I had." Mouth tight, he glanced over to where Peabody murmured to Pachai. "We have a policy not to lend money to anyone in the program, but to try to find another way to help, to guide them to help themselves. I never imagined . . . The three of them together should have been safe. God knows, each one of them had experience on the street, handling themselves."

"I have to ask where you were between one and four this morning."

"Yes. I . . . Well, here. I was here."

26

"That's a lot of midnight oil to burn."

"What I'm working on, it's — I believe — at its tipping point. I worked until after two, then bunked on the sofa in my office."

"Did you see or speak with anyone during that time?"

"No. I sent Ken and Pachai home about eleven, I think it was. You can ask them, or check the log-outs. Marti left earlier. I spoke with Arianna . . . I'm not sure, I'd have to check the 'link log. Maybe ten or ten thirty before I sent the boys home."

"What are you working on?"

"A serum to counteract deep and chronic addiction and substance abuse. It will treat the craving on both a physical and psychological level, quiet the violence of that need during withdrawal, and after."

"There are medications for that already."

"Medications that basically substitute one chemical for another. I'm attempting to work with natural ingredients that will trigger the chemistry in the brain and the body to return to the levels prior to the addiction. A rebalancing, we'll say."

He rubbed at his temple again, the same two fingers on the same spot in the same circular motion. "Is there anything I — we — can do for them now? Contacting family? I can't remember the details of that, but Arianna will have it. With the burial, memorial? Anything?"

"We'll be notifying next of kin. I'll need to talk to Ms. Whitwood, and as soon as possible. First I'd like to speak with your other assistants."

"Interns," he corrected automatically. "Marti Frank and Ken Dickerson are here on intern scholarships.

Sorry, it hardly matters. I want to tell Ari in person, face-to-face, not over the 'link. We lose patients, Lieutenant. To their addiction, to the violence it often generates, or the physical abuse it causes. But this? This comes very, very hard."

"Is she in the Center now?"

"Yes, she should be in session now. I'll go up, tell her."

"If you'd tell her I want to speak with her before we leave, I'd appreciate it."

"Yes. I'm sorry to meet you this way. I'm just . . . sorry."

Eve let him go, and decided to take the redhead first.

"You got the picture," Eve began.

"Yeah. It's a really ugly picture."

"Were you close to the victims?"

"I hate that word. Victim." She folded her hands together on her lap as if she wanted to keep them still. "It's overused."

"It is in my line of work."

"Yeah, I guess. Not especially close. I liked them. Jen in particular. She was just so damn likable."

"You work in the lab. Do you get friendly with a lot of people in the program?"

"There's interaction. It's part of it. There's a communal eatery on-site, so a lot of times staff's eating with patients and recoverings. When work allows, we're encouraged to attend sessions or lectures. It's more than lab work, especially for Justin. It's our whole life, and understanding who and what we're working for. You're going to find out," she added. "I know how it

28

works. My brother was a junkie, favored Jazz laced with Zeus. He favored it a lot right up until he OD'd. He made my life, my mother's, my father's, hell. I hate the junk, and it took a long time before I stopped hating the junkie."

She glanced over her shoulder. "With Ken it was his father. Came into it late, you could say. Started with prescriptions after a car accident, escalated until he'd destroyed his marriage, did time for smacking his wife and Ken around, ended up on the street where he stabbed somebody to death for twelve dollars and a wrist unit. He died in prison when somebody returned the favor."

Eve connected the dots. "And Pachai?"

"Childhood friend. They were tight, like brothers. The friend played around with recreationals, liked them too much until he was flying on Ups and Bounce, crashing on Chill. Then he was just one more OD when Pachai found him dead — two days dead. Justin wants people invested who work for him, people who know all the sides, all the layers, and have a reason to be here."

"He wants it personal."

"Yeah, and it is." She looked over at Pachai, then down at her folded hands. "This happening to Jen and the others, people who had a real shot at redemption, who really put it all into kicking it? That's personal, too. For all of us."

"Understood. If you know how it works, you know I have to ask. Where were you between one and four this morning?"

"In bed." Her gaze tracked up, met Eve's. "Alone and asleep. I had a date, but it didn't go anywhere. I got home just after midnight. I've got a roommate, but she had a date and it did go somewhere. She didn't get home until six this morning."

She gave Eve a narrow look. "Anyway, from what you said, how they were killed? The three of us would've had to go batshit together, break in to that place, and kill them like a pack."

"That's a thought, isn't it? I appreciate the time. If you think of anything, contact me or my partner."

Eve moved on to the last.

"Ken Dickerson," he said. "Did they maybe get attacked on the street?" He watched Eve with horror and hope. His face, pale and thin, showed signs of fatigue. "Maybe they ran," he continued, in a voice that hitched in a battle against tears. "And the people who attacked them went at them when they got to the building."

"No."

"It just doesn't seem real," he murmured, rubbing at his damp, tired eyes. "I feel like I'm going to wake up and none of this happened."

"How well did you know the victims?"

"I . . . God. I don't know. To talk to. Not like Pach, but we hung out a couple times. My uncle manages a Slice, and I helped Jen, then Coby, get jobs there. I mean, I asked my uncle if he could give them a try. He's good about giving people a chance."

"Did you ever go to the place they were staying?"

30

"Once. The restaurant's close to where I live, so I go in a lot. I walked back with Jen and Coby one night. My uncle gave them some food. And we hung out." He smiled a little. "It was nice."

"Did they own 'links?"

He blinked in puzzlement. "Sure. Everybody has at least one 'link."

"Do you know anyone who'd want to hurt them?"

"I don't see why anyone would. They were harmless. They didn't have anything, didn't hurt anybody. Jen was studying so she could do secretarial work. She wanted to work in an office. That's not much to ask."

No, Eve thought. It wasn't much to ask.

When Justin came back in, he looked drained. "If you could give Arianna a few minutes, she'll meet you in the Meditation Garden."

"All right."

"Is there anything more we can do?"

"Not at this time."

"Will you keep me — us — informed?"

"I can do that. If anything occurs to you, anything at all, let me know." She signaled Peabody, who put her hand on Pachai's shoulder before rising.

"Arianna Whitwood, down in the gardens," Eve told her. "Did you get anything?"

"He was in love with Darnell," Peabody said as they headed down again. "He didn't hesitate to tell me, or that he thought maybe she felt something back. No alibi, but he gives off this gentle, kind of sweet vibe. I can't see him slaughtering three people."

"On the other hand, he and everyone in that lab knew all three vics, and where they were squatting. At least two of them — and I'd add Rosenthall as a third — had been there, knew the setup. That weighs. There are going to be others who knew them and the setup from Get Straight, and Slice. This wasn't random."

"No. Random doesn't fit."

"Because?"

"Oh boy, a quiz. Deliberate break-in through the back, and the other killers — because I can't see it being one guy — got into the front, attacked them in a frenzied but systematic manner. Wrecked the place, but as far as we know took nothing but their 'links — and at least one of them had the protective gear, so no blood on his — or their — clothes. It's most probable they brought the weapons — a knife, scalpel, and some sort of bludgeoning tool — with them. Prepared, premeditated, and target specific.

"Did I pass?"

"Not bad." They passed through an atrium on the main level and into the burgeoning gardens. "Not bad at all," Eve said with a look around.

"Totally mag. Peaceful. Kind of Zen. Look, butterflies." A smile broke over Peabody's face. "Butterflies just make you happy."

"They've got that buggy body and those creepy little antennas. People don't think about that because they get distracted by the wings. I always wonder if they have teeth. They must have tiny, sharp little teeth."

"You're not spoiling my happy."

32

Eve took the path marked Meditation Garden, angled through blossoms and butterflies. She saw Arianna on one of the stone benches, the diamond on her left hand on fire in the streams of light. She wore a leaf-green suit with a foam of lace and high, razor-thin heels of the same color that showcased long legs. Her hair, a rich, nutty brown, was wound up in some complicated twist that left her exceptional face unframed. Everything about her said classic and class, and reminded Eve of Mira.

At their approach, Arianna turned her head. Her eyes, a color caught somewhere between green and brown, sparked with anger.

She rose.

"Lieutenant Dallas. I'd hoped to meet you, but not like this. Detective Peabody. Can we sit?" She did so, folded her hands again. "I wanted to talk to you here. I'd hoped to find some quiet here. But not yet."

"You were the therapist for all three victims," Eve began.

"Yes. They would have made it. I believe that. On a professional and personal level, I believe Coby and Wil would have made it. I know Jen would have. She'd come so far in such a short time. She'd found the quiet."

"Dr. Rosenthall used that term. *The quiet.*"

"Yes, I guess I picked it up from him." Arianna laid a hand on her heart. "Addiction is never quiet. It's violent or sly or seductive. Often all three. But Jen found her quiet and her strength, and was helping Coby and Wil find theirs."

"Other addicts, not making such progress, might resent them for theirs."

"That's true. They would have told me if anyone was pressuring them, threatening them. Jen was addicted to heroin, preferred it in the mix they call Chill on the street. She often bartered her body for hits. Her mother was the same, her father was her mother's dealer — she thinks."

"She did some time in the system," Eve put in. "Juvie, group homes, foster homes."

"Yes. She had a troubled, difficult childhood. Jen ran off when she was sixteen, and continued that troubled, difficult life up until nearly four months ago when she woke up after a binge. She'd lost three days, and came back to herself covered in cuts, bruises, filth, her own vomit in some basement flop with no recollection of how she'd gotten there. She got out, began to walk. She thought of the next score, thought of just ending her life, and she came to Get Straight. Instead of walking on, trying for the next score, or ending her life, she went in."

"This wasn't her first try at rehab."

"No." Arianna turned her head to meet Eve's eyes. "She'd had three court-assigned rehabilitations, and none of them took. This time, she chose. She walked in on her own. She was ready to be helped, and they helped her. Justin and I were there that day. She often said that was the beginning for her. When we met."

Arianna looked away again as her voice roughened.

"Withdrawal is hard and painful, but she never gave up. She brought Coby in. We encourage recoverings to sever ties with people who are part of their addiction, but she wouldn't listen. She saved Coby, simply because she wouldn't give up on him either, and then Wil. They loved her, and their love for her and each other proved stronger than the addiction. That's a kind of miracle. And now . . ."

"Did they tell you about anyone who concerned them, who gave them any grief, put any pressure on them to use again?"

"No. None of them had any family, no one they were close to or had contact with, not for a long time. They formed friendships, associations at the Center, and at Get Straight. They were still in the honeymoon stage, so happy to be where they were, so happy to have each other."

"Were they intimate?"

"No, not sexually. Jen and Coby had been, if you can call it intimacy, when they were both using. What they'd formed now was a family, so they lived that way. For Jen, sex had been that bartering tool, or something to do with another addict. She'd become desensitized about sex. I think she was beginning to feel normal and natural urges. She was attracted to Pach — Pachai Gupta — and he to her. But neither of them moved on it."

"How can you be sure?"

"She would have told me. Honesty had become a vital tool for her in recovery, and she trusted me. They'd made a vow — Jen, Coby, and Will — to abstain for six months, to focus on themselves as individuals. Coby joked about it. He was funny, sharp. He'd used that charm and wit to survive on the streets. Now he used it to keep himself and his friends steady. Wil went the more spiritual route. He'd lived with his great-grandmother until she died, and she'd taken him to church. He'd started to go back. Jen and Coby went with him a few times, but more for friendship than interest."

"What church?"

"Ah . . . Chelsea Baptist."

"Where else did they go routinely, do routinely?"

"They liked to hang out at the Twelfth Street Diner, drink coffee, and talk. They all put in time at Get Straight, attending meetings, taking on chores — cleaning, organizing donations — that's part of the program. They attended group there, too, as well as here. They'd see a vid now and then, but primarily they worked — saved their money toward finding a place to live — concentrated on the program, studied. Or Jen did. She was taking a business class."

"You gave them permission to live in the building?"

"Yes. Justin asked me, and we thought it would give them a breather, allow them to live on their own, save, stay close to the Center. The stipulation was they had to keep the place, and themselves, clean. They did."

"You visited them there?"

"Either Justin or I would drop by once a week. Spot-check," she said with the first hint of a smile. "We trusted them. But you can't trust the addiction."

"Arianna!"

The sharp call sliced through the quiet garden. A man, tall, his dark hair cropped close to a tanned face, hurried toward them. His eyes, a green as sharp as his voice, were all for Arianna. Ignoring Eve and Peabody, he grabbed her hands, got to his knees.

"I heard what happened. What can I do for you?"

"Eton." Tears shimmered in her eyes. Eve saw her bear down against them. "I was going to tell you myself, but I needed to speak with the police. Lieutenant Dallas, Detective Peabody, my associate, Eton Billingsly."

"The police." He shot Eve a disgusted look. "At a time like this?"

"Murder usually brings the cops."

"It's hardly necessary to interrogate Arianna at all, and particularly before she's had time to process."

"Okay. Let's interrogate you. Where were you between one and four a.m. this morning?"

He blustered. Eve couldn't think of another word for the sounds he made or the look on his face as he sprang to his feet. "I'm not answering any of your insulting questions, and neither is Arianna."

"Oh yeah, you are," Eve corrected, "here or at Cop Central. Your choice."

"Eton." Arianna rose. "Stop now. You're upset. The police are trying to find out who hurt Jen and the boys, and why."

"They'll hardly find out here, with you." He took her hands again. "Justin should never have allowed it."

"Justin doesn't *allow* anything." Gently, but deliberately, Arianna drew her hands away.

"You're right, of course. But it's natural to want to shield you from this kind of ordeal. I know how much you'd invested in these recoverings."

37

"I haven't heard an answer yet, Mr. Billingsly."

"*Dr.* Billingsly," he snapped at Eve. "And at that time of the morning, I was home in bed."

"Alone?"

"Yes."

"What was your relationship with the victims?"

Perhaps due to the fact that his face went red, Arianna answered for him. "Eton is one of our psychologists. He specializes in hypnotherapy. The process can help them through withdrawal, give them focus, and can often help them bring the root of their addiction to the surface."

"So, did you do the 'you're getting sleepy' with the victims?" Eve asked him.

"Yes."

"And?"

"As Arianna can tell you, they were making excellent, even exceptional, progress."

"When's the last time you had contact with them — each of them?"

"I'd have to check my book. I can hardly remember off the top of my head."

"Do that. Did you ever visit the building where they were living?"

His lips thinned. "No. Why would I? Instead of wasting time here, you should be out on the street, looking for the maniacs who did this. It's obviously the result of violent addicts, people they associated with before they began the program."

"Nothing's obvious at this point. You've been very helpful," she said to Arianna.

38

"Can you let us know when . . . Justin and I would like to arrange a memorial. We'd like to arrange for their remains."

"Arianna," Billingsly began.

"Eton, please. It's little enough."

"I'm required to inform the next of kin," Eve told her. "I'll be in touch once I have. You have transcripts of your sessions with them. They could help me. Doctor-patient privilege doesn't apply when the patients are dead."

"I'll have them sent to you this afternoon. I'll show you the way out."

"We've got it, thanks."

As they walked away, Eve glanced back. Eton had her hands again, his head bent toward hers as he talked rapidly.

"Asshole," was Peabody's opinion.

"Big, flaming asshole with a big, flaming temper. Looks like he keeps in good shape. Bet he puts in plenty of gym time. And he wants Arianna Whitwood for his own."

"Oh yeah, and she doesn't want him for hers."

"That's a pisser for him. I bet she gave the vics a lot more of her time, attention, and affection than she gives Billingsly, which is another pisser for him."

"Killing the hell out of them doesn't change that. Would be a pretty murky motive."

"Maybe, but I really hate him already. Plus, hypnotherapy. Who knows what he's up to with that?"

"Why didn't you ask for his transcripts?"

"Because he wouldn't give them up, not without a warrant, which you're going to put in the works while we head over to Get Straight."

"Oooh, that's going to be another pisser for Billingsly."

"I can only hope it's not the last."

CHAPTER
FOUR

They got little more from Get Straight but confirmation of everything they'd heard before, and more grief. Even as they stepped out into the air holding the first faint hint of fall, Eve's com signaled. She recognized the first on scene on her screen.

"Officer Slovic."

"Sir, we dug up a wit claims she saw someone near the rear of the crime scene, and observed him stuffing something in the recycler where we found the bloody protective gear."

"That's a break. How good a look?"

"She claims a good, solid one. There's a streetlight, and she states she saw him clearly, and he was dancing."

"Sorry?"

"That's her statement, Lieutenant." Eve heard the shrug in his voice. "Her description's pretty strange, but she's sticking to it, and doesn't strike me as a whack job. Her apartment's got a good view of the area, and she was up walking her kid — kid's teething. She's a short-order cook on parental leave. We got her on the canvass."

"What did she see?"

He cleared his throat. "A monster. Possibly a demon."

"Officer Slovic, are you actually wasting my time on this?"

"Sir, I wouldn't, but she gave details, she had the time down, and she admits it sounds crazy."

"Give me the details."

"Male, medium build — she thinks — dark hair, wild and stringy." He made the throat-clearing sound again. "Greenish skin, red, bulging eyes, contorted features, and prominent teeth, wearing a black cape and carrying a black satchel."

"And this green, red-eyed monster was dancing in the streetlight."

"And laughing, sir, in what the wit describes as a wild, guttural laugh. I believe her, Lieutenant, I mean about what she saw. It could be the subject was wearing a mask or a disguise."

"Yeah." Eve heaved out a sigh. "Will she work with an artist?"

"She's anxious to."

"Contact Detective Yancy at Central, and get her to him."

"Yes, sir."

She shoved the com into her pocket. "A green, red-eyed, cape-wearing monster."

"Or possibly demon," Peabody put in and earned a sneer. "I'm not saying I believe in monsters and demons, but somebody hyped up on Zeus, say, convinced he is one, gets in the gear to top it off. Since the wit only saw one man, and the evidence leans

42

toward one man — he'd have to be hyped on something. Zeus not only makes you crazy, but it deadens you to pain, pumps the adrenaline."

"Maybe. We'll see it through." She checked the time. "I want you to go by Slice, talk to the boss, the coworkers, and do the same at the twenty-four/seven. You can round it off with the diner they used as a hang spot. Maybe they had some trouble last night, or somebody followed them home. I'm going to swing by the morgue, see what Morris can give us. We'll hook up back at Central."

"I'd sure as hell rather go to a pizza joint than the morgue. Want me to bring you a slice?"

"No . . . maybe. Yeah."

Eve slid behind the wheel and headed for the morgue.

Zeus was a good fit, she thought, but not a perfect one. It fit the violence, the frenzy of it. But not the calculation. Still, a blend . . . and some enterprising soul was always coming up with a new and improved in the illegals game.

Flying on Zeus, a man could hack, beat, choke — and laugh his ass off while doing it. But he couldn't plan — costume, satchel with weapons and protective gear, gloved or sealed hands. She didn't expect the sweepers to gift wrap the killer's prints for her.

He'd broken in through the back window, Eve thought, bringing the scene back into her head. Need a tool for that, in the satchel. Climb in, nice and quiet — something else that didn't fit the Zeus, not pure Zeus.

Bathroom, back room all neat and tidy, so the killer had moved straight into the front of the shop and the vics.

Target specific, premeditated, planned. She was sure of it.

Motive was a murky area.

She considered, rejected, fiddled with various theories through downtown traffic, then let them simmer as she walked into the white tunnel of the morgue.

Morris wore a gray suit and a strong red tie. The choice cheered her a little. His wardrobe rarely varied from black since the murder of his lover. The band twined through his braid of dark hair matched the tie.

His long, clever eyes met hers over the open body of Jennifer Darnell. Through the speakers, a sax wailed out a jazzy riff.

"I see you got me a triple-header."

"The monster did it."

"Not difficult to believe, given the condition of these young people. There's internal abuse, self-inflicted from years of illegals ingestion, poor diet. They lived hard for their short time. I found signs of recovery and reversal. If they'd lived and kept clean, they should have done well enough."

"Were they keeping clean?"

"Knowing you'd ask, I ran and rushed the tox screen first, and they were. Their last meal, which I assume they shared about midnight, was pizza, a diet cola for the girl, straight cola for the boys."

"Sexual activity, consensual or forced?"

"No. Victim one — in order of TOD — suffered multiple broken bones and ribs, some of them postmortem. COD would be a fractured skull. He'd literally had his brains bashed in. By a bat or pipe, some three inches in diameter, and extreme force. I found some paint flakes in the wounds. I've sent them to the lab."

"Head blow first?" Eve speculated.

"From my reconstruction, which is still preliminary, yes. A blow here." Morris tapped the side of his hand diagonally over his right temple. "It would have knocked him out cold. It's unlikely he felt the rest."

"Small favor."

"Victim two, multiple stab wounds inflicted with a jagged-edged blade, some four inches in length. Not a hunting or carving knife. More likely an inexpensive meat knife. The tip broke on bone, and that's at the lab as well. He was stabbed first center of the chest, two strikes, and once in the abdomen. Again, from my prelim, the rest of the wounds came several minutes later."

"Incapacitate both males."

"And her. As in your notes, she was struck with the same bat as killed her friend, across the knees, shattering her kneecaps. The ear, eye, and tongue were removed postmortem, and with a smooth, sharp blade — a scalpel would be my opinion. And it was done with precision. Do you know how many are responsible for this?"

"One."

Morris's eyebrows shot up. "One? You never fail to intrigue." He looked over the bodies again. "The damage here, the strength, the sheer energy it took to beat the first vic was considerable. On the second, the stab wounds are very deep, very forceful, and there are eighty-five holes in that unfortunate boy. That also takes strength and energy. Considerable endurance."

"And when he'd finished there, he still had enough to manually strangle — correct?"

"Yes," Morris confirmed, "he used his own hands."

"To manually strangle the third, which also takes strength. And still after that, he had it in him to break chairs, tables, basically wreak havoc. He ended it, according to the wit we're working with, by dancing down the sidewalk."

"Then he has a powerful constitution, probably chemically enhanced. He enjoyed this." Morris laid a gentle hand on Jennifer Darnell's head. "I'm not Mira, so that's simply a dead doctor's take. But you and I see, every day, what one human being is capable of doing to another. This one enjoyed himself."

"Yeah, and when they have that much fun, they want to do it again."

She headed to Central. She needed to review her notes, write an initial report — harass the sweepers and the lab for theirs — start her murder board and book. And she wanted a look at the wit, or at least Yancy's sketch.

Somewhere in there she wanted to carve out some time to do a good, solid run on Eton Asshole Billingsly.

She smelled cookies the minute she stepped into the bullpen, caught the scatter of crumbs on Jenkinson's shirt, watched Baxter stuff the remains of one in his mouth before he offered her a big smile.

"Nadine's in your office, LT."

"Pathetic. Pathetic that a bunch of cops, fat-assing at their desks instead of out taking down bad guys, can be bribed with cookies."

Jenkinson shot up a hand. "We got one, Dallas. Reineke's walking him down to lockup. I'm doing the fives."

"With cookie crumbs on your shirt."

He brushed at them hastily as she turned away to stride to her office. Where Nadine Furst, reporter extraordinaire, lounged in her visitor's chair, nibbling on a cookie and working on her PPC.

Saying nothing, Eve lifted the lid of the bakery box on her desk, took out a fat chocolate chip. "What do you want?"

"A man of amazing sexual prowess, great sensitivity, stupendous abs, and the face of an angel. Toss in a wicked sense of humor and stupendous wealth, who adores the very ground I walk on. Oh wait, you already have him."

Eve bit into the cookie.

"Second choice?"

Nadine fluffed back her streaky blond hair, smiled her feline smile with her cat's eyes glinting. "I heard you caught a messy one."

"That's right. I don't have anything to give you. I haven't put it together yet."

"Three victims, beaten, stabbed, and strangled, recovering addicts with a connection to the Whitwood

Group — killed, in fact, on property owned by same. The Whitwoods are always a strong story."

"The victims are the story."

"I know." Nadine's smile faded. "They were young, trying to turn things around. Are you looking at gang and/or illegals-related murders?"

"I'm looking at everything, everyone."

"Including the Whitwoods, and the very dreamy Justin Rosenthall."

"Including." Nadine, Eve calculated, was always a good source. "What do you know about Eton Billingsly?"

"He's a dick."

"I got that much."

"Is he a suspect?"

"Nadine, it's too early."

"Well, I hope he is, because he's, as I said, a dick. Comes from money. Not quite on the Whitwood level, but he's got a fat portfolio. He also seriously courted the lovely Arianna, who fell head over skirt for Rosenthall — who is not a dick. I don't know much about him, but I can find out."

"I'm working on it." Eve took another bite of cookie. Damn fine cookie. "What else do you want?"

"You're just back from closing a big one in Dallas. Isaac McQueen — the second time you took him down. It's a hot story, Dallas. Him coming after you, abducting one of his former victims. I want you to come on *Now* and talk about it."

Eve set the cookie aside. Damn fine or not, her appetite dried up. "I'm not going to do that."

Before she could say anything else, Nadine held up a hand. "And I'm not going to press you. I had to ask."

"It's not like you to give up so easy."

Nadine recrossed her legs. "A couple of years ago when you and I hooked up over the DeBlass case, I did a little research. I like to know who I'm working with."

Eve said nothing.

"It's not easy getting much background on you, but I know you were found in Dallas when you were a child, and you'd been . . . hurt. The reporter wants an interview, Dallas, but the friend won't push. Friendship's stronger than a story."

"Okay." And it was.

"When you get something on this new case, maybe you can give me a heads-up."

"Maybe I could. You should contact Bree and Melinda Jones," Eve said as Nadine rose. "You should go to Dallas, where it happened, talk to them there."

"I intended to contact them." Nadine angled her head. "An on-location special? That's not bad. Some of it in the apartment where he kept Melinda Jones and the girl, some in the hotel suite where he came after you. No, that's not half-bad. I've got to go."

At the door, Nadine paused, glanced back. "Dallas, anytime you want to talk to the friend, about any of it, the reporter will step back."

"I appreciate it."

Alone, Eve turned to her 'link and contacted another friend. She was shuffled directly to Dr. Louise Dimatto's v-mail, left a message asking for a meeting.

Rising, she programmed coffee, then began to set up her board. She'd work better with the visuals.

When she finished, she started her report.

"That's particularly gruesome," Roarke said from her doorway.

Nadine had been right, Eve thought, in her summary of him. Oh, she'd left a few things out, but all in all. He did have the face of an angel, a fallen one, with the wings well-singed, but that only made him more compelling. That and those wildly blue eyes, the silky black hair. He wore one of his sharp business suits, but there was no asshole vibe here as with Billingsly.

This was power, success, sex, and danger all rolled into one streamlined package with Ireland gilding his voice.

Still.

"What are you doing here?" she demanded.

"I had business nearby, and took a chance I'd see my wife. And here she is. This is new," he said, looking at her board again.

"Caught it this morning. Oh, Justin Rosenthall and Arianna Whitwood say hi."

"Is that so?" He shifted his gaze back to her. "What would they have to do with this?"

"That's a question. How well do you know them?"

"Not that well." He ran a hand absently over Eve's shoulder as he moved closer to the board. "Surface, socially, charitable foundation events sort of knowing. He's intense without being preachy, and she's dedicated without being tiresome. And they both put their time and effort into their particular cause."

"Eton Billingsly."

"Git," Roarke said, using his childhood slang in insult.

"Maybe you can elaborate on that later, but right now I have to —" She broke off, answered her 'link.

"Dallas."

"I've got the sketch, Lieutenant," Yancy told her. "I think you're going to want to see it."

"On my way."

She clicked off, rose.

"Why not have it sent to your comp?"

"Because he's going to want to explain it to me." She thought of the description. "You can tag along."

"Why not, since it's unlikely I can talk you into a late lunch or early dinner." He flipped open the bakery box, helped himself to a cookie. "This will have to do. I haven't had time to monitor the police reports," he added as they walked. "Tell me about the case."

She did as they used the glides to get to Yancy's level.

"A strong Whitwood-Rosenthall connection," he commented. "As I said, I don't know them well, but I can't see them involved in that. Unfortunately, I can't see Billingsly involved either. Certainly he wouldn't stoop to getting his hands dirty."

"People who work with addicts, day in, day out, sometimes end up using themselves. Maybe one, or more than one of them, gets in too deep. Newly recoverings can be like converts. Fervent. One of them finds out, threatens to spill it. Reputation's ruined, the Center blackened, blah, blah.

"Whoever did it had some medical training," she added. "Morris confirms the amputations weren't the work of an amateur."

"Any number of people at the Center and Get Straight would have medical training."

"Yeah, and I'm going to look at all of them."

She moved through Yancy's division, straight to the glass cube where she saw him and a woman in her early thirties with a baby on her lap.

Yancy gave Eve a nod.

"Cynthia, this is Lieutenant Dallas. LT, Cynthia Kopel — and Lilian."

"Thanks for coming in Ms. Kopel."

"I'm happy to. I only wish I'd contacted the police last night, when I saw him. But I just thought it was some crazy. I didn't know about those people until Officer Slovic knocked on the door today."

As she spoke, the baby sucked heroically on one of the plugs parents used to keep babies from screaming — as far as Eve knew.

"We appreciate your cooperation and information. Can I see the sketch?"

Yancy exchanged a look with the witness, and Cynthia sighed. "It's what I saw. I know how it looks, but it's what I saw."

Eve held out a hand for the printout. And when Yancy gave it to her, looked at the face of a monster.

CHAPTER
FIVE

The crooked jaw accented a twisted mouth with teeth long, sharp, and prominent. A thin nose hooked over it. The eyes bulged and gleamed red against skin of pale, sickly green. Hair fell in oily twists over a wide forehead, over ears with a defined point, nearly to the shoulders of a swirled black cape.

"I know how it looks," Cynthia repeated, bouncing the baby on her knee either out of nerves or habit. "I know I sound like a nutcase, but I'm not. I got a good look because he was dancing around in the streetlight, like it was a spotlight on a stage. Just weird. Well, I thought — after it scared the hell out of me for a second — just some weird guy. But then when the police came and said those three people had been murdered right across the street . . ."

"Maybe he dressed up for it," Eve considered. "Theatrics."

"I know he was creepy. And that laugh." Cynthia shuddered. "It was this maniacal laugh, but low and deep — and kind of raw. Like he had something stuck in his throat. After he stuffed something in the recycler, he bent over, his hands on his knees, laughing and laughing. I started to go wake up Reed — Lilian's daddy — but then he — this guy — left. He went up the street — spinning around so the cape he was wearing twirled."

She let out a sigh. "You see all kinds of strange stuff and people in the city, and half the time you barely notice or get a kick out of it, you know? But this was . . . Well, it made the hairs on the back of my neck stand up."

"When you see something like this in the middle of the night outside your window, it would spook you," Eve commented.

The tension in Cynthia's face eased. "I didn't think anyone would believe me. I felt stupid, but then those three people, I had to report it once I knew. However he looked, how could he be laughing and dancing around after killing them? He is a monster." She drew the baby closer. "On the inside, he's exactly how he looked. Evil."

"I know how it looks, too," Yancy said after he'd walked Cynthia out. "But she was solid, Dallas."

"Yeah, I got that. I don't think we'll be issuing a BOLO on this face at this time, but she saw what she saw. The attitude fits — the laughing, dancing around, the theatrics. There was definite glee in the killings. So he dresses up for it, adds some punch." She frowned over the sketch. "He strangled Darnell face-to-face. Is this what he wanted her to see? Adds more fear, but it's not as personal if she's seeing this mask, this disguise, and not him."

"Are you certain she knew him?" Roarke asked.

"Oh yeah. They knew each other. He knew all of them. Ear, eyes, tongue. What did they hear, see? What was he afraid they'd say? So . . . send me the file copy," she said to Yancy. "We'll start checking costume shops, theaters."

"If it's makeup," Yancy told her, "he's a pro *and* an expert. If it's a mask of some kind, it's damn good, so it'd cost large."

"Yeah. And that should help. Nice job, Yancy."

"Here to serve. Strangest sketch I've ever done, and I've done some strange."

"Have you considered a combination?" Roarke asked as they walked back. "That he has some sort of deformity and played it up. The jaw — if your witness has it right — it looks severely dislocated."

"I'm going to be working that angle, but nobody I've interviewed so far has any kind of facial deformity. You can't hide something like that. If it's a medical condition . . . I'm waiting for Louise to tag me back. Maybe she'd have some ideas on that. Or Mira. I need to walk this through with Mira."

When they stepped back into the bullpen, Peabody hailed her. "Not much to add from Slice or the twenty-four/seven or the diner. I'm writing it up. Hey, Roarke. Lucky I brought back a personal pie. Maybe Dallas will share with you."

Eve picked up the takeout, passed it to Roarke. "Maybe she will. Did you see anybody like this?" She offered Peabody the sketch.

"Whoa. Seriously?"

"Yancy thinks the wit's solid, and as I talked to her myself, I agree."

"Part demon, part monster, part human. He's like a mutant."

"He's like somebody in costume," Eve corrected. "Start running down this look. Theaters, costume outlets. See if you can find anything that fits." She started to dig out money for the pizza.

"You got the last one," Peabody told her.

"I probably did. And let's see if we can find anyone connected to the center or Get Straight who's involved in theater or theatrical makeup. Costume parties," she added. "Places like the Center have fundraisers like that, right? Where they make people dress up like idiots, then squeeze them for donations."

"I doubt they think of it in quite those terms," Roarke considered. "But, yes."

"We'll look at that. If you get anything close to a hit," she told Peabody, "let me know."

She went back in her office with Roarke. "Go ahead," she said, gesturing at the take-out box. "I want to try to get a meet with Mira."

She sat and began chipping away at the scales of the dragon at Mira's gates. "Ten minutes," Eve insisted. "I've got three DBs."

"And Dr. Mira has a full schedule today."

"Ten minutes," Eve said again. "For this." She angled so her 'link captured the murder board.

"In thirty minutes," the admin told her. "Don't be late."

"I won't."

Sampling the pizza, Roarke wandered over to her board. "You know, you could contact Mira directly."

"Yeah, but it's not right. Channels are channels for a reason, even when they're annoying."

"I suppose. You've discounted this being done by someone from their past? An addict, a dealer."

"Not discounted." She tried the pizza herself. "But the probability's low any of them knew someone back then who had the skill to surgically remove body parts. I think he was on something when he did — the frenzy, the strength and endurance, then laughing and dancing. So even flying he had skill, a steady hand. Add to it, Darnell's been out of that for nearly four months and wouldn't be tough to track down. If she'd known something that threatened someone with this skill, wouldn't he have dealt with her before? For four months she's been immersed in the Center and the program. It's somebody attached to that."

"I can't fault your logic. I rarely can."

Her 'link signaled. "Dallas."

"Dallas, I was in surgery." Louise, still in scrubs, mask dangling, came on screen. "I just heard. I can't quite believe it."

"You knew them."

"Yes. I'm actually Jen Darnell's physician of record. I do her monthly exams. Did," she corrected. "I'd see her often when I did a rotation at either the Center or Get Straight. And Coby, too, in the last few months. I met Wil recently. He hasn't been in the program as long."

"How well do you know Rosenthall and Arianna Whitwood?"

"Very well. They were in Haiti helping to set up a new clinic when Charles and I got married or they'd have been at the wedding."

"Eton Billingsly."

Louise's pretty face pruned. "He's an excellent therapist and a complete jerk."

"I need to talk to you about this."

"I've got another surgery scheduled. It's minor, but they're already prepping the patient."

"Have her and Charles meet us for drinks," Roarke suggested and got a blank look from Eve.

"Here." He simply nudged her aside. "Hello, Louise."

"Roarke. I didn't realize you were there."

"Why don't you and Charles meet us for drinks after work? You and Eve can discuss what needs to be discussed."

"Yes, I think that would work."

While Roarke set it up, Eve turned back to her board. She liked Louise and Charles, but wasn't sure how she felt about her interview with a source turning into a social hour.

What the hell.

"Find somewhere to meet up near the crime scene," Eve said, and gave Roarke the address. "I want to go back over it."

"There." Roarke turned away from the 'link when he'd finished. "Now you can talk to Louise, revisit your crime scene, and have a little time with friends. Interlude on West Eleventh, between Sixth and Seventh. At five, or as close as you can make it."

He skimmed a fingertip down the dent in her chin. "It's efficient."

"I guess it is."

"I've got a meeting shortly, so I'll see you there." Leaning down, he brushed his lips over hers. "Take care of my cop," he told her, then left.

It should have weirded her out, Eve mused, sharing pizza and good-bye kisses, making dates for drinks in her office. It did, she admitted, but not as much as expected. Her gaze landed on the bakery box, narrowed.

She said, "Hmmm," and, picking it up, walked out. She ignored the noses that came up sniffing as she passed through the bullpen, and caught a glide to Mira's office.

The admin, busy on her comp, glanced up with a stern frown. "You're early."

"Then I'm not late." Eve set the box on the desk. "Thanks for clearing time for me."

Stern turned suspicious as the woman lifted the lid of the box a fraction, then more as she peered in. "Cookies? You brought me cookies?"

"They're good. I had one. Is she free now?"

Still eyeing Eve, she tapped her earpiece. "Lieutenant Dallas is here. Of course. You can go right in."

"Thanks."

"Are these a thank-you or a bribe?" the admin asked as Eve moved to the door.

"They're chocolate chip." Pleased with herself, Eve stepped into the calm of Mira's office.

Mira smiled from behind her desk. Maybe it was a shrink thing, Eve considered, thinking of Arianna. The warm looks, the pretty, feminine suits, perfect blend of color and jewelry.

"I know you don't have much time."

"Enough, I hope. Have a seat." As Eve took one of Mira's blue scoop chairs, Mira came around the desk, took the one facing. "I looked over the data, the crime-scene photos. My first question is, how sure are you there's only one killer?"

"Very. We have a wit who saw him at the rear of the building, where he broke in. She worked with Detective Yancy." Eve took out the sketch, offered it.

"Well." In her placid way, Mira studied the sketch. "Now I have to ask, how good is your witness?"

"Again, I have to say very. I figure he geared himself up for it, added the drama. The wit says he danced in the streetlight, laughed his ugly ass off. My sense of the scene is frenzied glee. He had to be on something because killing three people that dead takes endurance."

"I agree." Mira tucked a lock of sable-colored hair behind her ear as she continued to study the sketch. "Theatrical, confident, organized. He knew where to break in, came prepared, and was able to kill, with extreme violence, three people, alone, and in a relatively short amount of time. Endurance, yes, and rage."

She shifted, met Eve's eyes with her own quiet blue ones. "I agree with your assessment that he has some sort of medical training. The amputations were skillfully done. I believe he'll keep these trophies, these symbols.

60

His victims are no longer able to see, hear, or speak of him."

"But they had, prior to their deaths."

"Almost certainly. They knew each other. Dancing, laughing, so yes, he enjoyed himself. He can celebrate — and in the light, perhaps hoping he'd be seen. Spotlighting after his success.

"He envied their friendship," Mira continued. "Their bond, and their happiness. He won't make friends easily, won't feel that bond. He most likely lives alone, feels underappreciated at his work. He's skilled. The elaborate disguise tells me he wants to be noticed, and doesn't feel he is, not enough. Nothing is enough. He wants what others have — friends, family, community — and at the same time feels superior to them. He's better than they are. 'Take out the trash,' he wrote, in their blood. That's what he made them. And it amused him. He's a series of contradictions, Eve. Two people — perhaps more — in one. You have a violent sociopath under the influence of a strong illegal. He's both controlled and out of control, canny and reckless. He has a god complex battling with low self-esteem, a bitter envy, and has found satisfaction and personal delight in killing."

"He'll do it again."

"As soon as he can."

"This face. Under the makeup or the mask, whatever it is, could he have a deformity? The jaw's extreme."

"Yes, I see that, but a deformity such as this? He'd be in constant pain. It would be all but impossible for him to eat. His speech would be garbled. As someone with medical training, and connections, he would certainly have had this repaired."

"A recent injury, accident?"

"Possibly," Mira considered. "But again, I can't think of any reason it wouldn't be treated. If, for some reason, he refused to have it treated and is dosing himself with painkillers and other drugs, it might explain the frenzy, the duality in his profile. But why would anyone endure the pain of this, the social stigma? And it contradicts, again, his confidence, his need to be seen as superior."

"It must be faked. Peabody's running down costume shops, theaters." Eve paused a moment, changed angles. "Do you know Justin Rosenthall and Arianna Whitwood?"

"Yes. Arianna's an excellent therapist. A bright, compassionate woman. She and her parents have done a great deal, not only in research and application on addictions and rehabilitation, but they built their Center with the purpose of treating the whole person. Physically, emotionally, mentally, spiritually. They turned a personal tragedy into a great gift."

"And Rosenthall?"

"Very skilled, remarkably gifted. More intense than Arianna, I'd say. It seems to me — though I don't see or socialize with them often — she's softened that intensity. Before Arianna, he was much more of a loner, and rarely stepped away from his work. Not unlike someone else," Mira said with a smile. "With her, he remains skilled, gifted, dedicated to his work, but he's happier. And not capable of murdering three people like this."

"Everyone's capable," Eve stated.

"Yes, you're right. All of us are capable under certain circumstances of extreme and violent behavior. We control it, channel it — in some cases medicate it. Justin's a doctor, dedicated to healing, a scientist and man of reason. The person who did this rejects reason and humanity. He's given himself a monster's face. Humanity means little to him."

"Okay. How about Eton Billingsly?"

"A skilled therapist, and an enormous pain in the ass."

Eve had to grin. "I don't think I've ever heard you call anybody a pain in the ass."

"I don't like him so it's hard to be objective. He's a pompous snob who sees himself as perfect. He's rude, annoying, and full of himself."

"A god complex?"

Mira's eyebrows rose. "Yes, I'd say. You wonder if he's capable. I don't know him well enough. He's skilled — he has an MD, and would have done some time with a scalpel before he focused on his specialty."

"Hypno-voodoo."

Mira let out a quick, exasperated laugh. "I know you're suspicious of the technique, but it's valid, and can be very effective. Billingsly certainly wants to be noticed and rewarded and praised. But . . ." She studied the sketch again. "It's very difficult for me to envision a man like him deliberately making himself hideous. He's also vain."

"Something to think about, though. I appreciate the time."

"I'm happy to give it. Tell me how you are."

"I'm fine."

"You haven't been back long. How's your arm?"

Eve started to dismiss it, then settled on the truth. "A little sore in the morning, and by the end of the day. Mostly good, though."

"That's to be expected with that kind of injury. Nightmares?"

"No. Maybe just being back in New York's enough. At least right now. Isaac McQueen's back in a cage where he belongs. That doesn't suck. I'm not thinking about my mother, what happened there," she said before Mira could ask. "Not yet. It's done, and right now I'm okay with it."

"When and if it's not, you'll talk to me?"

"I know I can. That's a pretty big start, right?"

"Yes, it is."

Eve got up, started for the door. "Is she like you?" she asked. "Arianna Whitwood?"

"Like me?"

"That's the sense I got from her. She made me think of you. Not just because she's an attractive female shrink. It was . . . I don't know, a sense. If she is like you, then she's got no part in this. And thinking that, I hope to hell Justin Rosenthall doesn't, because you believe she loves him. I hope he's clear."

"So do I."

"I'll let you know," Eve said, and left.

CHAPTER
SIX

Eve glanced over at Peabody as she walked back into the bullpen, got a shake of the head.

So no luck, yet, on masks or makeup. She went into her office, got coffee, then sat at her desk, put her boots up, and studied the board.

Everybody liked Rosenthall; nobody liked Billingsly. Instinct dictated a push on Billingsly — and she intended to listen. But she'd give a little push on the good doctor as well.

Arianna Whitwood. Beautiful, rich, smart, dedicated, caring. The good daughter, and again, the good doctor.

Didn't that make an interesting triangle? Billingsly wanted her — and didn't bother to (ha-ha) disguise it. Rosenthall had her.

And what did that have to do with the three vics?

They were Arianna's. Her patients, her investment, her success — at least so far. Rosenthall's, too.

Maybe Arianna had given them too much time, attention, made too big an investment. A man could resent that. She sometimes wondered why Roarke didn't resent all the time, the attention, the investment she put into the job.

But there weren't a lot of Roarkes in the world.

Maybe the three vics — or any one of them — overheard Arianna and the good doctor going at it over her work, that time and attention again. Hey, bitch, what about *me?* Shouldn't I be the center of your world? Maybe he'd lost his temper. Couldn't have the gossip mills grinding that one.

And no, just not enough for that kind of slaughter.

Maybe the vics, or one of them, overheard the two doctors-in-love arguing because Rosenthall was sampling product. Experimenting. That's what you did in a lab. You experimented. Maybe he'd developed a problem of his own during those experiments. Now that, combined with being found out, could lead to bloody, vicious murder. Could be Arianna didn't know. Can't have her find out he's become what he's supposed to cure.

That could play.

Or, onto Billingsly. He pushed himself on his beautiful associate, and again one or all of them saw the incident. Possible.

Or the annoying doctor fooled around with a patient, maybe — hmm — maybe tried a move on Darnell. Rejected, humiliated, worried she'd tell Arianna. He'd lose any chance with the woman he wanted, and his license to practice.

That could play, too.

But none of it played very well. Maybe she just needed to fine-tune a little.

For now, she read over Peabody's notes on her interviews at Slice and the twenty-four/seven, the diner hangout. Nothing buzzing there, Eve thought, but continued as Peabody had started or completed a number of deeper runs on the players in those arenas.

Rising, Eve got another cup of coffee, then started deeper runs of her own on Rosenthall, Billingsly, Arianna, Marti Frank, Ken Dickerson, and Pachai Gupta.

Gupta came from some wealth, and an upper-class social strata, and she considered the fact that his parents, also doctors, had worked with Rosenthall years before.

Now Gupta had the plum position of the renowned doctor's lab assistant on a major project. Couldn't something like that make a career?

How would Gupta's upper-class parents feel about him pining for a recovering addict? Possibly he wanted to keep that on the down low, and possibly Darnell wanted to go public.

Possibly.

Both Marti Frank and Ken Dickerson came from the ordinary, and in Dickerson's case the rough, with his dead addict of an abusive father. Both had excelled in school, she noted. Frank top of her class in college — on a full scholarship. Dickerson third — accelerated path. He'd graduated high school at sixteen, college — again on scholarships — at nineteen, and straight into medical school.

And they were both still on scholarships, she noted, in the intern program at the Center.

She brought the lab setup back into her head. Working together on the project, she mused, but they'd seemed very separate, hadn't they? With Rosenthall center. Neither Dickerson nor Frank had gone to Gupta when he'd broken down.

So not friends — not especially.

Competitors? Didn't you have to have a competitive streak to come in first in your class, or in the top tier with acceleration?

And was it interesting, she wondered, or frustrating to learn that all six of them had sufficient medical training to have performed the amputations?

She'd eliminate the females, except one of them might have acted in collusion. Dead low on the list, she decided, but it felt too soon to eliminate.

All of them knew the vics' location. None of them had alibis for the time in question. All of them knew and/or interacted with the vics. All of them had access to drugs and could easily put their hands on the protective gear.

She picked her way through the data on each suspect, added to her notes, her board. When the sweepers' initial report came through, she pounced. More paint flakes, some black fibers from the window casing, some hairs — no roots. All sent to the lab.

None of the victims' 'links had been found on scene. So he'd taken them. Taken the 'links, she mused, but not the money. Fibers on the windowsill, footprints in blood. So he'd only sealed his hands, or worn gloves.

And walking through the blood, that was just stupid. Amateur hour. If they found the shoes, they had him.

First kill, she thought. She'd make book this had been his debut.

Time to circle back.

She walked out to Peabody. "I'm going back to the scene."

"Okay. I'm not getting anywhere anyway."

"No, you keep at it. I'm going to talk to Louise after, then work from home."

"I'm serious about getting nowhere." Peabody huffed out a breath, shoved at her hair. "I've talked to the top costume shops — and some costume and theatrical makeup designers in the city. What I get is, sure the skin color's no problem; hair, no big; nose, teeth, you bet. But the eyes? Every one of them tells me if they used apparatus like that — to make them bulge out, or appear to, and turn that red — it would hamper vision. Same with the jaw."

"It was dark, even with the streetlight. Middle of the night. Maybe the wit exaggerated some."

"Maybe. A couple of the people I talked to were all juiced up about it, trying to figure out how to make it work. I've got them promising to experiment, see what they can do. But nobody's got anything like this. Not in any sort of mask, or doable with makeup and prosthetics. Nothing that would allow the person wearing it to see clearly, speak, or laugh the way the wit described."

"Keep at it anyway, because it is doable, as it was done."

"What if he's some kind of freak?"

"Peabody."

"I didn't say demon or monster. Like a circus freak, you know? A contortionist or a freak show type. He looks like this — or something like this and he just pumped it up."

"Circus. That's an angle. I'll work that at home. Not bad, Peabody."

"You'd kick my ass if I said monster."

"Keep that in mind if you become tempted," Eve warned, then headed out.

She thought of makeup, freaks, altered appearances as she drove — and had a brainstorm. "Contact Mavis Freestone, pocket 'link."

Contact initiated.

"Hey, Dallas!" Mavis's pretty, happy face filled the dash screen. "Say hi to Dallas, Bellorama."

Instantly, the baby's chubby, grinning face replaced her mother's. "Das!" she cried with absolute joy, and pressed her wet lips to the screen of the pocket 'link.

"Yeah, hi, kid. Kiss, kiss."

"Slooch!"

"Right. Smooch."

"Make the sound, Dallas," Mavis said offscreen.

Eve rolled her eyes, but complied with a kissing sound. Bella squealed with yet more delight.

"Playtime." There was some shifting, giggling, then Mavis came back on behind the film of Bella's slobber. "Why didn't you tell me you were going to Dallas?" Mavis demanded.

"I didn't have time. It was —"

"We're going to chit some serious chat about this."

"Okay." With Mavis, it would be okay. "But later. I need you to — can you wipe your screen off? You look like you've been licked by a Saint Bernard."

"Oh, sorry. So what's the up?" Mavis asked as she whipped out a cloth and polished the screen.

"I'm going to send you a sketch, and I need you to get in touch with Trina, show it to her."

"Why don't you just send it to her?"

"Because I'm busy."

Mavis angled her head. Her hair, a curling mass of gold-streaked red today, bounced. "Coward."

"I'm a busy coward. I don't want her giving me grief because I didn't rub some shit on my face, or in my hair. Or listen to her tell me I need my hair cut or whatever. I've got something hot, and she might be able to help."

"Give me the goods. So I finished my gig on the vid," she said as Eve ordered the sketch accessed and sent.

"What vid?"

"Nadine's vid — your vid. *The Icove Agenda*. It's mag to the nth they wanted me to play myself. And the chick playing you? Man, they made her a ringer. I got wigged when I — Holy shit on a flaming stick!"

"Shit," Bella echoed happily in the background.

"Oh hell — hello," Mavis muttered. "I swore in front of the baby. But holy you know what, this is too totally scary. I'm scheduling my nightmare right now."

"Sorry. I need to know what it takes to make somebody look like this."

"A pact with Satan?"

"With makeup and prosthetics, and that stuff. Trina knows that crap."

"I'll be passing it on — and getting it off my 'link just in case it has the power to materialize."

71

"Come on. Other angle. You did some carny work."

"Back in the day, sure. Always plenty of marks at a carny."

"Ever see anything like this? Freak show-wise."

"I saw plenty of mega weird, but nothing like this. You wouldn't ask unless it — he — whatever — killed somebody. He looks like he's born to kill. Jes — jeepers," she corrected. "I got bumps of the goose all over. I'll tag Trina now, so I don't have to wig alone."

"Thanks. Let me know."

Eve pulled over at the curb in front of the crime scene.

She unsealed the door, used her master. And stood inside, left the lights off. Not as dark as it would've been, she thought. But there was a streetlight, enough for some backwash.

Still, he'd had to know which mattress each vic slept on. He'd moved with purpose, with a plan despite the ferocity.

She moved straight through to the back, opened the window, climbed out.

And yeah, the building across the street had a good view of the window, the sidewalk, the recycler. Eve imagined the killer dancing and spinning in the spot of the streetlight, laughing.

Spinning and dancing up the street, Cynthia had said. So he didn't care about being seen. A vehicle nearby? Or a hole to crawl into. His own place?

If he'd taken a cab, the subway, a bus? Even in New York somebody would've reported it. All of the lab rats lived within blocks. Both of the doctors and Arianna had vehicles.

Eve turned back to the window. He jimmies it, she thought — quiet now. No dancing and laughing, not yet. Climbs in.

She followed the steps, easing in, sliding down to her feet — left fibers behind. Opens the satchel for the protective coat.

Some boxes in here, she noted, and tidy piles of old materials — but he doesn't bump into them. He's been here before. And he walks right into the front.

As she did, the door started to open.

She had her weapon out, trained. Then hissed when Roarke stepped in.

"Damn it."

"I'm the one with a stunner aimed at me. I get to say, 'Damn it.'"

She shoved it back in the holster. "You're not supposed to pick the lock on a crime scene."

"How else would I get in? Your vehicle's outside, and the seal's broken. I knocked like a good civilian, but you didn't answer."

"I was out the back window."

"Naturally." He stood where he was, looking around. "What an unholy mess. The crime-scene records never have quite the same impact."

Since he was here, she'd use him.

"He jimmied the window, rear, quietly stepped around the stuff back there — in the dark or near dark. Not much would come through the window — it's grilled — from the streetlight. But he doesn't wake them."

"He'd been in here, and back there, before."

"Yeah. Knew just how to navigate, and knew where each one slept. Leads with the bat." She swung. "Cracks Vix across the side of the head where he lay. He's the lucky one. I doubt he ever woke up. Changes to the knife." She mimed switching hands. "Puts it into Bickford's chest — two blows, and another in the gut. Fast. Bickford might've made some sound, tried to call out, but his lung's punctured. Now it's time for Darnell."

"She'd have woken, don't you think?"

"Bash, slice, movement. I think she woke up before he'd finished with Bickford. Got up, either tried to run or tried to fight. He uses the bat, breaks her kneecaps. Maybe she screamed — nobody heard — or maybe she just passed out or went into shock. But he went back to Vix, beat him into jelly. Blood's flying everywhere, bones snapping, shattering. He put the protective gear on in the back room, but blood's on his face. It feels warm, tastes hot. He loves it. He wants more, so he goes back to Bickford with the knife and stabs and hacks. Over eighty times."

Eve shifted. "She tried to drag herself away. See, the blood's smeared on the floor there from her knees, from her trying to pull herself away. But she's in terrible pain, in shock, in hysterics. He's laughing now because this is so much fun. Just better than he'd ever imagined. And now it's her turn."

She could see it, all but smell the blood.

"He says her name. I bet he said her name, and his. He wanted her to know him. It's face-to-face, it's his hands on her throat so he can feel her pulse going wild, then slowing, slowing, slowing while her eyes bulge and her body beats itself against the floor. While that pulse stops, and her eyes fix, and her body goes limp."

"Christ Jesus, Eve."

"That's how it happened." Inside she was as cold as the images fixed in her head. "That's close, anyway. He's not done. It's too funny and thrilling. He doesn't use the knife. He takes a scalpel out of his satchel because he takes pride in the work. Now he makes a point. An ear, an eye, her tongue. They're a trio, aren't they, like the monkeys. Hear no, see no, speak no."

"Evil," Roarke finished. "Because he is. What you've just described is evil."

"Maybe, maybe even to him. But he likes it. Likes the taste of evil, the smell of it. He just can't get enough, so he breaks the place up, what little they had. Destroys it. He stages them against the wall. Then he uses their blood to leave us a message."

Roarke studied the wall. "It took time to do that. His letters so carefully formed. Not dashed off, but clearly printed. He gave it some thought."

"He's so clever, a real joker. Dr. Chaos. I bet he slapped his knees over it."

She paused a minute. "Arianna said something. How they'd found their quiet. Especially Darnell. That addiction steals the quiet. That's what he brought back. The unquiet. The chaos. So that's the name he picked."

She walked away, into the back. "He takes off the protective gear. Turns it inside out to keep the blood off his clothes, and he climbs back out, shuts the window. He laughs, and he dances, just so full of the fun of it he can't contain it. He stuffs the gear in the recycler, properly disposing of it like he tells us to do with the bodies. A little clue, so we'll be sure to find it. And that has him doubled over with laughter. Then he dances away, high on the unquiet. Dr. Chaos had the time of his life."

"Did you learn any more from this re-creation?"

"Maybe. Yeah."

"Then you can tell me about it over the drink I find I want very much right now."

CHAPTER
SEVEN

Eve looked around the bar as they went in. Quiet and cozy, with a neighborhood feel, she observed. A couple of guys sat at the bar, deep in their brews and conversation. She bet they were regulars, bet the seats of the stools all but carried the imprint of their asses.

The bartender, bright, young, female, joined in with them, idly swiping the bar with a rag as she laughed at something they said. A couple sat at a table — had a first-date, drink-after-work-to-see-how-it-goes look about them. Another four had a booth, scarfing down bar chips while they held one of those quick, coded conversations of intimate friends.

Roarke took a booth, smiled at her over the table. "Satisfied?"

"About what?"

"That you won't have to arrest anyone in here."

She smiled back. "You never know."

She opted for a beer when the waitress came over, and Roarke held up two fingers. "Now, as we're a bit early, tell me what you learned back there."

"It was the girl. It was Jen. She was the primary motive. He wanted her to see what he did, how he killed the others, took away what mattered most to her in the cruelest way. She was the easiest kill of the three, but he saved her for last because she was the most important. Then he killed her with his hands, so she could see his face and he could see hers. The others didn't matter as much, except for their connection to her. He wanted her, and she said no — or worse, didn't see him as a man."

"He didn't rape her. I looked at your board."

"It had gone past sex or rape as power and control, and he got off on the killing. But taking the body parts — they'd seen or heard something he couldn't afford them to talk about. Whatever it was, it was recent."

She waited until the waitress served the beers. "See that group over there." She lifted her chin toward the booth of four. "Two guys, two girls. But they're not couples."

"Aren't they?" Roarke said, enjoying her.

"Look at the body language. They're tight, but it's not sexual. Pals. And they never run out of conversation. Blah, blah, blah. They talk all the time, hang all the time. When they're not together, they tag each other. He took their 'links because he got that, he knew they connected that way when they weren't together, and had to conclude they'd talked about whatever they'd seen or heard via 'link."

"All right."

"He worked alone. He doesn't connect, he doesn't have that closeness with anyone. So that bumps the two female suspects down the list for me. It wasn't Arianna Whitwood or Marti Frank. They may know something, may not know they know it, but this one had to have all the fun for himself. He's smug, and a show-off, which is why I like Billingsly just on principle."

"Arianna said no to him," Roarke pointed out.

"But he still believes he can get her. She's also on his level. How humiliating would it be for a man like that to want an addict, a squatter, a *nothing*, and be rejected by her?"

"That's a great deal for a second look at the crime scene."

"But not enough. Here's Louise and Charles."

Roarke stood, greeting Louise with a kiss, Charles with a handshake.

As Charles, former licensed companion turned sex therapist, slid in beside his wife, he grinned at Eve. "How's it going, Lieutenant Sugar?"

"I've got three bodies and a short list of suspects. It could be worse. Sorry," she said to Louise. "Insensitive."

"No. We both deal with death all too often, but at least I come into it when there's still a chance."

"You look tired," Roarke commented.

"Long day. Good day," she added, "as I didn't deal with death."

Both she and Charles ordered a glass of the house white.

"What can I tell you about your short list of suspects?"

Eve drew out the sketch, laid it on the table. Puzzled, Louise leaned closer. "We've still got a month till Halloween."

"This is who the witness saw outside the crime scene."

"It's a hell of a disguise," Charles commented. "Why would anyone want to dress up, be that noticeable when doing murder?"

"Maybe it added to the thrill. We're not having any luck on replicating the disguise, and Mira says it's unlikely he could tolerate the jaw — broken or dislocated that way."

"Now you have two doctors telling you that. This is extreme." Louise tapped a finger, tipped in pearly pale pink, on the sketch. "There would be airway blockage, difficulty breathing, speaking, eating. There should be considerable swelling, but I don't see any in this sketch. The pain would be enormous. And the eyes certainly aren't natural. Not just the color. Hyperthyroidism can cause the eyes to bulge, but I've never seen anything that severe. And the skin? I'd diagnose multiple organ failure at worst, anemia at best. He had to fake all this."

"Hey, I saw that guy." The waitress paused as she served the wine.

"When?" Eve demanded. "Where?"

"Last night. Well, this morning. You don't forget a face like that," she added with a laugh.

"Exactly what time? Exactly where?" Eve drew out her badge, laid it next to the sketch.

"Oh. I guess he wasn't just a weirdo. I had the late shift last night, so I didn't leave until after two. I live on Jane, right off Greenwich Street. I did some yoga when I got home. It relaxes me. I don't know exactly, but it was probably about three fifteen, three thirty or

80

thereabouts, when I finished. I heard this weird laughing, and went to the window. I had it open, and I saw this dude here sort of skipping down the sidewalk across the street. You see all kinds, you know, so I didn't think anything of it. I saw him jump up, swing on the pole of the streetlight, waving this black bag. I just thought, weirdo, shut the window, and went to bed."

"Which way was he going?"

"East, toward Eighth, it looked like. What'd he do?"

"Enough so if you see him again, contact the police." She hitched up a hip, dug out a card. "Contact me."

"Sure. Wow, a lieutenant. Homicide. Wow. He killed somebody?"

"Yeah. I'd like your name and address."

"Sure. Sure." Once she'd given it, the waitress hurried away.

"You scared the hell out of her," Charles said.

"She'd be smart not to walk home alone, and to keep her windows closed." She put the sketch away, sipped at her beer. "Do you know any of Rosenthall's lab people?" she asked Louise.

"No."

"Okay, we'll set them aside for now. Did Rosenthall ever move on you?"

"No! He was with Arianna when we met, then I was with Charles not long after. He's in love with Ari, and added to that, his work doesn't give him a lot of time for moving on other women."

"It doesn't take that much time. She's the one backing his research and work — or the Group is. If she cut him loose, it'd be a big loss."

"She's in love with him, and they're bonded over the work," Louise began. "If something went wrong between them, it would be a blow for both of them, personally and professionally."

"But scientists are easier to find than backers like the Whitwood Group. If his work's important to him."

"Essential, I'd say."

"Then he'd do a lot to protect it."

"Not this, Dallas. Never this. Not Justin."

"I'm going on the theory the three victims knew something about the killer. Something he killed to protect. Has Justin ever sampled product?"

"Absolutely not."

Okay, Eve thought, as long as Louise spoke in absolutes they wouldn't get anywhere on Rosenthall.

"How about Billingsly?"

"I can't say. I'd certainly doubt it, but I don't know him well." Louise smiled a little over her wine. "That's a deliberate choice."

"He put moves on you."

"He puts them on every female he finds attractive or believes can enhance his career. But Ari's the gold ring."

"How'd he react when you brushed him off?"

"Like it was my loss. He has a temper, but I've never seen anything to indicate he's capable of murder or real violence. He's rude and demanding, but from what I've heard, very good in therapy."

"And if Arianna cut him off — from the Center?"

"He has money of his own, and should have a lot of contacts. But it would be humiliating, and he wouldn't take it well. That's just opinion, Dallas. I have as little to do with him as possible."

"Okay, thanks."

"Not much help."

"You confirmed and elaborated on Mira's opinion on the killer's face. You gave me a few more details on two of my suspects, and meeting you here gave me another wit who tells me the killer went up to Jane before heading toward Eighth. That's pretty good over one drink."

When they left, Roarke took her hand as she walked. "You did very well, managing nearly a half an hour on non-work-related topics after your interview with Louise."

"I can talk about other stuff."

"You can, yes, but I know it's not easy when you're steeped in a case."

"The bar waitress was a stroke of luck. Heading toward Eighth. If it's either of the doctors, he's probably got a vehicle near there. If it's Dickerson, he goes one crosstown block to home. Gupta, north on Eighth for a block and a half to home. Nobody at Slice or Get Straight lives in that direction — and they don't fit anyway, but it's another negative on that group.

"Where's your car?" she asked when they reached the crime scene.

"I had it picked up so I could drive home with my adoring wife."

"Good. You drive." She took out her notebook, added the new information, new thoughts on the way home.

Roarke left her to it until she began to mutter.

"Is anybody really that good, the way everybody describes Rosenthall?"

"Some people have fewer shadows than others, fewer dark places. Others have more."

"And illegals speak to those dark places, make more noise so they spread. Everyone on this list connects to illegals. Lost someone to them, works with them, lives with them. The killer's a user — has to be. I don't have enough on any of them to require a drug test. Yet. But if I asked each of them, and they're clean, why wouldn't they cooperate?"

"General principles," he said as he drove through the gates of home. "But certainly worth a shot."

"I'll give it one tomorrow. Plus a scientist should be able to create an elaborate disguise."

She chewed on it as they walked inside where Summerset and the cat waited in the foyer.

"A monumental day," Summerset announced. "Home together, in a timely fashion, and unbloodied. Applause."

"If he actually applauded, the bones in his skeletal hands would break and crumble to dust."

Roarke just shook his head as Eve started upstairs. "The two of you really have to stop this love affair. I'm a jealous man. We'll get dinner in the lieutenant's office," Roarke added to Summerset.

"I'm shocked beyond speech."

"If only," Eve muttered.

"But before." Roarke took her hand again, turned her toward the bedroom. "Let's deal with that arm."

"It's okay."

"You're starting to favor it."

"It's just a little sore."

"Which means it's time for some of the physical therapy and treatment. Don't be such a baby."

She jabbed him with a finger. "You just want to get my shirt off."

"Always a bonus. Peel it off, Lieutenant." To make her smile, he leered. "And take your time."

So okay, it twinged a little when she took off her jacket, her weapon harness. Get it over with, she thought, and began the stretching exercises, working her range of motion as Roarke ditched his jacket and tie.

Her shoulder gave a couple of clicks as she stretched, punched out.

"It's coming along."

"So I see. Try to avoid actually punching someone for a few more days," he suggested as he got the topical cream from a drawer. He rolled up his sleeves as he crossed to her, then started to unhook her trousers.

"I knew it. All you think about is getting in my pants."

"With every breath I take. But for now, I just want a look at that hip. It was the worst of the cuts. Nearly healed," he murmured, tracing a fingertip along the edges where McQueen's knife had sliced. "Mira does good work."

"We've both had worse."

His eyes lifted to hers, held, and said a great deal. So she leaned into him a little, touched her lips to his.

"I'm okay."

"Nearly. Lose the tank and sit down. I'll finish you up."

She did as he asked, thinking he needed the tending as much as, maybe more than, she. Then his hands — he had magic hands — smoothed the cream over the ache, and she closed her eyes.

"Feels good. Really good."

"Mira credits your constitution, and your hard head, for the healing process. A couple more days, you'll likely be good as new. Tell me if I hurt you."

"You're not."

They hadn't made love since she'd been hurt — and she realized she should have figured why he'd been so careful with her, hadn't touched her that way, had avoided being touched by her.

"You're not," she said again and, opening her eyes, turned to him. "You won't." And took his hand, laid it on her breast. "Feels good," she repeated. "Really good."

"I only want to give you time to heal. In every way."

"I have it on good authority I have an excellent constitution. Let's test it out." Going with the instinct that told her they didn't just need the physical intimacy, but the fun that could go along with it, she tossed her leg over his lap, straddled him. "Get it up, pal."

Smoothing those magic hands down her sides, he smiled. "You're very demanding."

"You ain't seen nothing yet." She took his mouth, gave it a nice little bite as she ground against him. "There you are," she murmured.

86

"Well, you've left me no choice."

"A cock's always ready to crow."

He laughed, wrapped his arms around her. "Crowing's not what mine's ready for."

"Show me." She went to work on his trousers.

Amused, aroused, he watched her. "In a bit of a hurry, are we?"

"I've got to use you and get back to work, so no dawdling." Then she laid her hands on either side of his face. "Okay, maybe a little dawdling," she said and brought her lips to his again.

"I'm okay." She unbuttoned his shirt so she could press against him. Skin to skin, heart to heart. "I want you to touch me. I want you to be with me. I want you."

He could drown in her, he thought, every minute of every day he could lose himself in what she was, what she gave him, what she took. Now, with her warm and eager against him, he could drown himself, lose himself, and set his worry for her aside.

She didn't want him to be careful, but he would take care, of her injuries at least. He gave her the controls, took his pleasure from the rise of her passion, from the sprint of her heartbeat under his lips.

When she took him in, she laid her hands on his face again. Her eyes looked deep into his. "You're holding back. Don't. Don't hold back."

So he gripped her hips, careful to avoid the healing wound. And drove her as she drove him. Over the edge of that drowning pool.

With her brow resting on his, she fought to get her breath back. If anything twinged or ached, she didn't feel it. All she felt was peace.

"Did you really have business downtown today?"

"You're my business."

She lifted her head, looked at him again. "You have to stop worrying."

"That's never going to happen. But I will stop hovering, which I've been doing a bit of. I love you beyond the telling of it, Eve, and what you went through —"

"We. We went through it."

"All right, that's true enough. What we went through doesn't heal as quickly as a cut or a bruise."

"Working on it, though. Okay?"

"Yes." He pressed his lips to her healing shoulder. "Yes."

"Okay. Well, now that I'm done with you, I'm going back to work."

He sat where he was a moment as she got up, pulled the tank back on. "I feel so used. I find I like it."

She rolled her injured shoulder, nodded in satisfaction. "Always more where that came from, ace."

CHAPTER
EIGHT

In her office she set up a second murder board while the cat sat on her sleep chair and watched her. Through the adjoining door she heard Roarke talking on the 'link. Probably dealing with business he'd postponed during the hovering mode.

Better now, she decided. Both of them were better now. Not just the sex, but the understanding that came with it — or out of it. And the normalcy that went hand in hand.

"Nothing normal about that," she said as she studied the sketch. "Not a damn thing normal there."

She circled around to her desk, noticed that her message light was activated. She called up the message, and actually jolted when Trina's voice spiked into the room.

"Got the ugly bastard and the question. Could do the skin, hair, ears, nose, teeth, no prob. Could do the red eyes, but not so they look like red balloons coming out of the sockets. Couldn't do the jaw, not that crooked. The answer is I couldn't make anybody look like that, and I'm the best. You've got yourself a freakazoid, Dallas.

"You need a treatment — hair, face, body. The works. Mavis says she and Leonardo and Bella can come to your place for a visit on Saturday afternoon. I'll be with them, and bring my gear."

"Why," Roarke wondered, "do you look more horrified by that than by the face on your board?"

"She's coming. We have to stop her."

"Don't look at me. You could use a treatment."

"Hey." Though she was anything but vain, the careless comment gave her another jolt. "Insulting my hair, face, and body won't get you banged again anytime soon."

"You know very well I adore your hair, face, and body. You could use a massage, a relaxation treatment, and some downtime with good friends. In fact, so could I. I believe I'll contact Trina and have her bring another operative. I'll have a massage along with you."

"Traitor." She stomped to the kitchen for coffee, stomped back. "I'm not thinking about it. It's not Saturday yet. Anything could happen."

She wiped a hand through the air. "So. Everybody says it can't be done. Not costuming, not physically. But it has to be one or the other. If it's physical, maybe it's long-term. Something he's learned to live with. Peabody's circus freak angle. And if that's it, I eliminate everybody on my list."

She scowled at her board. "Pisser."

"Maybe one of your suspects hired the killings."

"I'm going to run probabilities on that, but it rips up the theory — and it's *more* than a theory — that the killer knew the vics. That it was personal."

"Maybe he just takes pleasure in his work."

"Crap. Crap. Crap. Somebody's wrong. Either the medical experts or the cosmetic/costume experts. I like it better if the cosmetics are wrong, but I've got to work it both ways. I've got to go back to the beginning."

"You can go back with me over a meal."

It usually helped to do just that, talk it through with him, bounce theories and angles off him. But this time, she felt she only circled without getting any closer to the center.

"I don't believe anyone looks like that," she said. "And if I decided to believe somebody did, I can't believe he'd stay off the grid. I ran that sketch through every program we've got and didn't get a single hit."

"Maybe it's more recent."

"The hypo-whatever, the multiple organ failure — and why isn't he dead, if so — and whatever trauma would cause the lower part of his jaw to be so dislocated it's nearly under his right ear? I don't think so. If he was a hire, how did anybody know about him — because he'd have popped if he was a pro, even semipro. If he killed them for himself, why doesn't anyone else know about him? Unless . . . maybe he's a patient at the Center. Maybe he's a kind of experiment they're keeping on the down low."

"As in botched?" Roarke twirled some seafood linguine on his fork. "As in mad science?"

"Mad, bad. Maybe. It's something to poke at. Maybe the vics knew him from before, and found out he was there, confronted the mad-bad scientist, or threatened to tell people on the outside."

"You don't like that very much."

"Not as much as one of them slapping gunk on their face, pumping themselves full of a Zeus cocktail, and whaling away, but it's another route to take."

She took it, working angles, running probabilities, reformulating, juggling through the pieces. When Roarke finally tugged her out of her chair hours later, she was more than ready to give it up for the night.

Clear her head, she decided. Let it simmer for a few hours.

Shortly after midnight, Eton Billingsly coded himself into Justin Rosenthall's lab using a cloned key card and a recording he'd made of Justin's voice.

He thought himself very clever.

It was time — past it — to prove to Arianna she was wasting her time and resources on Justin. The man was obsessed with this serum, and far too secretive about it in the last weeks.

Because he was getting nowhere, Billingsly concluded. The financial resources Justin wasted had become intolerable, particularly since they could and *should* be redirected to his own department. Once Arianna saw the truth, she'd rethink the relationship, and this wedding business.

He went directly to the main comp station, noted Justin had locked it down for the night.

But no problem, or very little of one. He'd worked with Justin long enough to know the man kept such things simple, so his assistant and interns could access data when needed.

Justin called it teamwork. Billingsly called it naivete. One day one of those underlings would steal data and take credit for whatever advance Justin managed to stumble onto.

But in this case, it simply made the job easier.

He tried various names as passwords, working patiently. At one point he thought he heard a sound, froze, turned to look around. Then shook his head at his own foolishness.

He continued until, inspired, he tried *Ari102260*. The date they'd chosen to be married. Sentimental fool, Billingsly thought as access was granted.

Quickly now, he scanned through file names.

UNQUIET. Justin's term for the core of addiction.

Before he could call it up, something crashed behind him. "What the devil —?"

He whirled, then froze.

"Some might call me that," the voice ground out, like rocks beneath a boot heel. "But I prefer Chaos. Dr. Chaos." The creature issued a deep, cape-swishing bow. "At your service."

"What kind of sick joke is this?"

"My kind. Sticking your nose where it doesn't belong, aren't you, Billingsly? Well, we'll just have to take care of that."

"I have every right to . . ." But he backed up as he spoke, with his heart hammering in his dry throat. "I'm contacting Security."

"Wanna bet?"

As Billingsly began to run, the creature let out a delighted laugh. Strength, speed, excitement poured through him as he leaped. Billingsly went down under him, screaming.

Chaos used the knife. But before the knife, he used his teeth.

And continued long after the screaming stopped.

The signal of her communicator pulled Eve out of a dream where she chased her killer while he danced down an empty street juggling an ear, an eye, and a tongue.

"Gross," she mumbled, then called for the lights at ten percent before she answered. "Dallas."

Dispatch, Dallas, Lieutenant Eve. Report to the Whitwood Center. See building security and officer on the door for access to Laboratory Six.

"Justin Rosenthall's area."

Affirmative. Possible homicide.

"Acknowledged. Inform Peabody, Detective Delia. Request that she meet me on scene as soon as possible. Has the victim been ID'd?"

Victim identification is not confirmed.

"I'm on my way. Dallas out."

She shoved at her hair, saw Roarke was already up, getting dressed. "Shit. Shit. You don't have to come. That's hovering, isn't it?"

94

"In this case it's sheer curiosity. The likelihood is it's your man, and since I'm awake now in any case, I'd like to see for myself."

It was quicker not to argue. Besides, he had an eye as good as most cops she knew. And drove faster and better.

"Inside job, what did I tell you?" She watched buildings whiz by on the way downtown. "It's one thing to break into the place on Twelfth, but it takes a lot more to get through the security they have at the Center."

At his noncommittal sound, she gave Roarke a narrowed stare. "For most people. Rosenthall's lab. He works late a lot. Shit, shit, *shit*."

She was out of the car the instant Roarke parked, flashing her badge at the NYPSD uniform and the building security officer.

"Lieutenant. Security Officer Tweed will take you to the scene. My current orders are to remain on the door."

"Has Detective Peabody arrived?"

"No, sir."

"Send her in when she gets here. She knows the way. Tweed?"

"This way."

"I know the way, too. Who found the body?"

"I did. I was doing a standard cam sweep, and I saw . . . a figure."

"Green, deformed face, red eyes, wearing a cape?"

"I wouldn't have believed it if I hadn't seen it myself."

"And you've got him on disc."

"Yeah. He was heading down from the second level, east, moving fast in a kind of — boogie. Part of me was

95

spooked, I admit. The other part figured somebody was playing a joke. But we have to check out any unauthorized activity. By the time I got to that sector — along with the other guard I'd alerted — he was gone. I went up, saw the lights were on in Dr. Rosenthall's lab, so I keyed in, and I saw . . . The place is wrecked, Lieutenant, and there's a body. It's male, but I couldn't tell who it was. The face, it's, well, wrecked, too. And there's blood everywhere."

"Okay." She nodded to the uniform outside the lab doors. "Key me in, Tweed, then I'm going to want those discs. The originals."

"I'll take care of it."

"And stand by," she told him.

Wrecked was a mild word for it, Eve thought as she scanned the area. Smashed comps lay on the floor on a sea of broken beakers, dishes, specimen bowls. The body lay faceup — what was left of the face. Blood stained the hacked and ripped clothes, spread over the floor, left its obscene abstract art on the sides of a counter.

And on the top, in blood, his message.

Memo to: Lt. Dallas.

Nobody liked him anyway.

You're welcome!

Sincerely, Dr. Chaos.

"It's Billingsly."

"How can you be sure?"

"That's the suit he had on this morning." She took a can of Seal-It out of her kit, used it, tossed it to Roarke. "This takes him off the suspect list."

"I doubt he'd feel grateful."

"What was he doing in here? He doesn't strike me as the type who'd come by for a late-night visit with Rosenthall, and this isn't his area. He's another floor up, in the other wing."

"He might have been lured here."

"Yeah, maybe. But it's late, way after hours. Why is he in the building, and where's Rosenthall? I need to know who keyed in before Security."

"Would you like me to see to that area?"

"Yeah, that would save time."

"His nose is gone."

"It sure is. What does that mean? Smell no evil? No, that's just stupid. To me it says nosy. You're nosy, Billingsly; now you're dead."

She turned as Peabody came in.

"Wow. Another day, another slaughter." Peabody eased out a breath. "McNab's with me. I had him start on Security. I thought maybe Roarke would be here, so we'd have two e-men on it."

"Then I'll go hook up with Ian."

"What do you see?" Eve asked Peabody when they were alone.

"I see Billingsly's off the suspect list."

Despite the circumstances, Eve smiled a little. "And?"

"He's been stabbed a whole bunch. It might even be more than Bickford, but it's hard to tell. He's missing his nose."

"What does that say to you?"

"It's another quiz. This time I want a grade. It says to me Billingsly won't be sniffing around anymore. Maybe around Arianna, maybe around something else — something lab related. The note's addressed directly to you this time, so he knows it's our case — and that Billingsly wasn't a popular guy around here."

"I'd say A minus."

"A minus?" Both insult and sulk piped through Peabody's voice. "I want A plus."

"For an A plus you'd need to observe, identify, and relate the teeth marks in the vic's face and throat."

"Teeth . . . oh jeez." Observing and identifying them now, Peabody swallowed hard. "He *ate* him."

"Just here and there. He's accelerating," Eve concluded. "This time blood wasn't enough. He wanted a taste of flesh." She scanned again, noted the open door on an empty cabinet. "Did the killer walk in on the vic, or the other way around?"

"If this is extra credit, I want a review of my earlier grade. Let me think." To help herself do that, Peabody looked away from the body. "I can't think why Billingsly would be here. He and Rosenthall aren't pals, and this isn't his area — not only sector-wise, but professionally. Maybe if Rosenthall asked him to come in — but I don't buy it. He's not going to do his competitor any favors. He'd come if Arianna asked him, but that puts her in this, and it just doesn't fit well for me."

Pausing, she made herself look at the body again. "If he came here — which, okay, obviously, he did — it was to get something on Justin, or screw with something, or poke around looking . . . Poke his nose in!"

Eve took the cloned key card and recorder out of Billingsly's pocket. Hit Play.

"*Justin Rosenthall.*"

"Billingsly tried a little B&E," Peabody commented.

"That's an A plus."

"Yay!"

"Billingsly keys in using the dummy card and the recorder. He's poking around. The killer is already here — looking for something, doing something, waiting for something. Billingsly sees him, and that's the end of Billingsly. The killer chews on him, stabs him, amputates his nose, wrecks the lab, takes time to leave the message, then boogies out. They've got him on disc, so we'll be able to track his movements."

"That's a break."

"For us, not for Billingsly." Eve opened her field kit again, crouched by the body. "Let's verify ID, get TOD."

"If there are bite marks, they should get some saliva, and the impressions, too," Peabody began.

"We got better." Eve lifted Billingsly's lifeless hand. "We got skin under the nails. Billingsly got some flesh, too."

CHAPTER
NINE

Eve put on microgoggles for a better look before she bagged the hand. "Tinted green flesh, so that's our guy. We'll get DNA."

"And see if one of our main suspects shows some recent scratches."

Eve looked up as Roarke came back in. "McNab's working with Security," he told her. "Everyone in the lab logged out, Rosenthall being the last at eleven twenty-six. The log shows Rosenthall swiping in again at twelve oh-seven, but the discs show Billingsly swiping in at that time, clearly entering alone."

Eve held up an evidence bag. "Billingsly had a clone swipe and a recording of Rosenthall's voice."

"Nosy becomes very apt. No one else entered the lab after the last log-out at eleven twenty-six except Billingsly. No one exited until your Dr. Chaos at one fifteen."

"Well, he didn't just materialize."

"TOD," Peabody announced before Roarke could comment, "twelve fifty."

"That's a lot of time between when Billingsly entered and TOD. It didn't take that long to kill him. Contact the sweepers, and the ME," Eve ordered, then, avoiding blood and debris, did another long study of the room, walked over to the break room area.

"Peabody! Get us a warrant for these lockers. Six, digital locks." Looking up, she studied the open ceiling vent. "There's his access. It's big enough for a man to get through."

"Low tech," Roarke commented. "But classic."

"I need the ventilation layout. But for now . . . boost me up."

Obliging, Roarke hooked his fingers together. With her foot in the hammock of his hands, Eve bounced up, gripped the edge of the open vent. "Yeah, the grille's in here. Maybe he initially planned to go back out this way." She took a penlight out of her pocket, shined it in the skinny ventilation tunnel. "Tight squeeze. I see some scuff marks. So he logs out, comes back in somewhere else. Through the health center area, maybe the visitor's lodging, pretty much anywhere. Scoots and crawls along. Pops out, then —"

"Are you going to solve the case while I'm holding you off the floor?" Roarke wondered.

"Hmm? Sorry." She jumped down. "Pops out," she continued. "Maybe gets into his gear here. Lockers, bathroom. Sweepers could find traces of the makeup. Would he be stupid enough to leave something in a locker?"

"Shall I open them?"

"When we get a warrant."

"Stickler," he said and made her smile.

"I could claim they're part of the crime scene, which they are, so the PA could probably hold that line. But a defense attorney would make noises, so a warrant keeps it clean."

She set her hands on her hips, turned a slow circle. "Was he meeting Billingsly here? In it together, there's a disagreement, death ensues. I don't like it. This guy works alone. Billingsly got nosy, then got dead. The killer wasn't expecting company. He came in for the serum, and he got it. Billingsly's a bonus round."

"Why didn't he go out the way he came in?"

"Too hyped up from the kill to care," she concluded. "By then, leaving where he'd be caught on disc — if he thought of it — just added some fun. Look at me!"

Peabody came to the doorway. "I tagged Cher Reo," she said, speaking of the APA. "She was about to call me a very bad name, but I showed her the body."

"Good thinking," Eve told her.

"She's all over the warrant."

"Okay. When the morgue gets here, I want the skin sent to the lab asap. I want that DNA the same way. I need something for a bribe. Something really good," she told Roarke. "For Dickhead."

Chief Lab Tech Dick Berenski wouldn't drag himself to work in the middle of the night for less than a first-class bribe.

"Two tickets, skybox, first game of the World Series, with locker-room passes."

"Excellent, but we're still in play-offs."

"Wherever it is — transpo included."

"Nice. I'll start with one, let him squeeze me for the second ticket — which he will. I'll tag him on the way to Security. I want to see those discs. Peabody, wait for the morgue and the sweepers. I want that skin hand-carried to the lab. And I want to know as soon as the warrant comes through."

In Security, Eve studied the screen, the movement, the face. She ordered magnification, ordered freeze, replay.

"Gotta be a new strain of Zeus, or something like it. Along with some serious prosthetics. Nothing's quite right about him. It's almost as if his whole body's disjointed."

She magnified again to study the hands. Gloved, she noted, with long, sharp nails slicing through the tips. Then went back to the face.

"He couldn't have taken those bites out of the vic wearing that gear. So he didn't put it on until after the kill. Or he can manipulate it, because the bites had puncture marks like those pointed incisors he's got. What is his deal?"

"Totally freak show," was McNab's opinion.

Eve glanced at the e-man, and Peabody's cohab. He wore his long blond hair in a tail secured with silver rings that matched the half dozen hanging from his earlobe. His skinny frame vibrated with color from the many pocketed baggies in Day-Glo orange that picked up the zigs in his shirt.

The zags were nuclear blue.

"You're wearing that getup and talking freak show."

He grinned. "Easy to find these pants in the dark."

"It'd be easy to spot them on Mars in the night sky with the naked eye."

"They blind the bad guys," he claimed, still grinning. "Anyway, Dallas, it looks real. This guy, I mean. He looks real."

"Nothing about this guy looks real," she corrected. "I want you to take this in to EDD for a full anal."

She looked down at her com when it signaled. "Warrant's in. Let's open those lockers."

"You're not going to like this," Roarke said as they walked back. "But I agree with McNab."

"Yeah, I figure those pants could blind somebody if they stared at them too long."

"Something I try to avoid. I also have to agree with him that your killer doesn't look as if he's wearing a disguise."

"Because it's a combination. Disguise and some kind of powerful drug."

"How does he blink?"

That put a hitch in her stride. "What?"

"If his eyes aren't real, if he's using devices for the size, the shape, how does he blink? He looked directly at the security camera at several points, and his eyelids closed and opened. He smiled, if you can call it that. His jaw shifted, his mouth turned up. And we both saw him contort his body in impossible ways, and move at considerable speed."

He did have a damn good eye, she thought.

"If he's a scientist — and he damn well is — he's figured out how to devise something, and he's taking something that boosts his adrenaline. Monsters exist," she added. "But they're flesh and blood. They're

104

human, just like the rest of us. It's what's inside them that's twisted. This guy isn't some Frankenstein monster."

"Actually, I was thinking of another classic. Mr. Hyde."

"You've got to lay off those old vids," she commented, and led the way to the lab.

"If you can believe a scientist can create devices and substances to disguise himself this way, why isn't it possible for that scientist to create something that causes him to *be* this way?"

"Because," she said as they approached the door, "appearing and being are different things." She paused outside the door. "Maybe — *maybe* — there's been something going on in this lab that's whacked. Something botched. And we're going to salvage Rosenthall's records and find out. But for now, we've got a killer on a spree, and none of my suspects pop out as a fucked-up science experiment."

"Maybe the more human face is the real disguise."

With that thought planted in her head, she walked into the lab.

Police business moved forward, with sweepers and the dead crew already at work. With Roarke she headed straight back to the lockers.

She thought of the destruction of the lab and the open, unbroken door of the serum lockup.

"No point in busting them open since you're here."

"None at all," Roarke agreed.

It didn't take him long. As he moved down the line of lockers uncoding the locks, she called Peabody in for the search.

And hit pay dirt in Pachai Gupta's.

Eve took out the silver pipe.

"Weighted it for extra punch. And he didn't even clean it thoroughly," Eve noted. "There's still some blood, some matter. It shows some nicks and dents where it hit bone."

"He loved her — Darnell." Peabody shook her head. "It was all over him, Dallas. Love and grief, all over him."

"He wouldn't be the first to destroy what he loved. But this is so damn stupid, so careless. Steal the serum by unlocking the cabinet rather than busting it up. Then just leave one of the murder weapons in your work locker?"

"A frame-up? It makes more sense to me," Peabody said. "I know I did the interview, and I hate thinking I missed anything, but a frame-up makes more sense."

"He's got this in the locker, but doesn't use it. Kills Billingsly, and unless he's really stupid, knows we'll search the lockers, knows we'll question the fact the serum cabinet was opened with its lock code. He's unstable, and the drug makes him more so, but he's organized. Takes care not to be seen coming in — but does murder, then shows himself."

"Because he wanted us here," Peabody concluded. "Following the bread crumbs to Gupta. No, not crumbs. Big, chunky hunks of bread."

"Reads that way. Seal it up, get the weapon taken to the lab for processing. And let's have all our players picked up, brought in."

106

She walked out with Roarke. "A frame-up, if that's what it is, that's human. So's screwing up and leaving evidence where it can be found, if that's what it is. Either way, with the weapon, the DNA, we'll lock it down."

"I have every faith. I'm going into the office."

"Now? It's . . ." She checked the time as they stepped outside. "It's shy of five a.m."

"Should I point out you've been working since shortly after two? I'll get my own jump on the day, and as I'm curious enough, I may come down to Central later, watch you lock it down."

"If you need the car, I could — Guess you don't," she added when a dark limo glided smoothly to the curb. "I'm going to hit the lab first, give Dickhead a push. A DNA match will save the innocent bystanders from a round in the box. Thanks for the bribe."

"Never a problem." He touched her cheek. "Take care, will you? This one gives me a very uneasy feeling."

"Too many old horror vids, and an Irish nature. I think I can handle some murderous scientist."

"Try not to punch him. You'll set the healing on that arm back."

She watched him drive away, then went back in to talk to the head sweeper and get Peabody for the trip to the lab.

Dick Berenski's ink black hair was slicked back over his egg-shaped head. Rather than his usual lab coat, he wore a multicolored floral shirt that would have made even McNab wince.

"What the hell are you wearing?"

"Clothes. It's five-fucking-a.m. I'm not officially on yet. And I want a bottle of single malt scotch for the game."

"We already agreed to terms."

"That was before." He shot her a sour look, and since the last time she'd seen him he'd been scarily sweet — and in love — she assumed there was trouble in paradise.

"Before what?"

"Before I got here and found Harpo pulling an all-nighter."

"Why is that my problem?"

"She's on your hair — first murder — and you're not going to like it." He played his spider fingers over his comp. "She'll come out here."

"What about my skin?"

"She goes first. And I want that scotch."

"Fine, fine, if you give me something I can use."

"Oh, I'll give you something."

Harpo, all spiky red hair and tired eyes, walked out from her section into Berenski's. "Yo," she said to Eve and Peabody, then dropped onto a stool. "You tell her?" she asked Berenski.

"I said you'd do it."

"Yeah, yeah, okay. So," she said, swiveling to Eve. "On one hand this is totally iced. On the other, it's majorly fucked."

"What is?"

"The hair. I'm the goddess of hair and fiber, and if I can't ID it, nobody can. And I can't."

"What do you mean?"

"Sorry, I've been at this all night. I'm a little wired on Boost." She gestured with the jumbo tube in her hand before she took a gulp.

"Have you tried the new black cherry flavor?" Peabody asked her.

"Yeah, but it's got an aftertaste. I'm pretty well hooked on the Lemon Zest. It's got a nice zing."

"I like Blue Lagoon. There's something about drinking blue that feels energizing."

"Excuse me," Eve said, brutally polite. "This talk of flavors and favorites is fascinating, but maybe we could take a moment to discuss — oh, I don't know — evidence?"

"Sure," Harpo said as Peabody cleared her throat. "I got hair from your crime scene. ID'd some from each of your vics, no prob. Got some not theirs, but no roots. So no DNA for you on that, but I started a standard anal. You want to eliminate animal — like a rat, or a stray cat, whatever. And I could — I figured anyway — give you some basics. Synthetic, human, if it was treated, color, and like that. But I can't, 'cause it's not."

"Not what, Harpo?"

"It's not synthetic. That's solid. But it's not exactly human and not exactly animal. It's sort of both."

"It can't be both."

"That's right." Harpo pointed a finger tipped with a metallic purple nail. "But it is." She glanced at Berenski for permission, then used one of the comps to call up her file. "What you have here," she said, tapping that bright nail to the image, "is human hair, and this" — she split the screen with a second image — "is ape."

"If you say so."

"Science says. See, on the human hair the cuticle scales overlap smoothly. On the ape hair, they're rough — they, like, protrude. Get it?"

"Okay, yeah. So?"

"So this —" Harpo added another image. "Okay, this is from your crime scene. It clearly shows characteristics of both — rough and smooth — on one strand. What you got here, Dallas, is mutant hair. It's like somebody mated a human with an ape, and here's the hair of the result."

"Give me a break, Harpo."

"Science doesn't lie. It screws up sometimes, but it doesn't lie. I ran this through everything I've got and did the same with the other strands the sweepers sent me. Same result. About two this morning, I gave up and tagged my old man —"

"Your —"

"My father's head of forensics at Quantico. Look, Dallas, it's not like I go running to Daddy whenever I hit a snag. In fact, this is the first time ever because it's way out of orbit, and he's the best there is — anywhere."

"Okay, Harpo, okay. What was his take?"

"He's stumped, just like me. This sort of mutation shouldn't be possible. But I've got hair — five samples — that says it is."

"So, you're telling me I'm looking for an ape-man? Seriously?"

"I don't know what the hell you're looking for, is what I'm telling you. Come on, Dickie, give her yours so she stops looking at me like they let me out of the ward too early."

Berenski folded his arms. "Harpo got what she got, and I got what I got. You got green skin."

"I know that, goddamn it."

"I mean green. Not makeup, not tinted. It's green down through the subcutaneous tissue. Your vic got some blood along with the flesh, and that's not right either."

"Green blood?" Eve asked, ready to be annoyed all over again.

"It's red enough, but it's not human. Not all the way. I get what Harpo got on the hair. A combination of human and ape. DNA's like nothing I've seen before, and I've seen it all. It is what it is," he snapped out before Eve could protest. "You've got some mutant freak running around killing people. I want some fucking coffee."

He shoved up, stomped away.

"His girlfriend dumped him a couple days ago," Harpo said. "He hasn't said it, but we figure. He's been hell to be around since. But he's right. It is what it is. My old man, he'd like to consult on this if you give him the nod."

Eve squeezed the bridge of her nose. "I'm going to get DNA from the suspects. When I do, can you match it to this?"

"Dickie's got DNA from the skin and blood the vic scraped off. He can match it if you get him the killer's.

111

You get hair, I can match it. But it shouldn't be a problem to find some half-ape guy with green skin. Right?"

"Jesus," was all Eve could think of.

Wisely Peabody kept her thoughts to herself. She managed to be wise until they'd gotten back in the car.

"You know Harpo's solid. And Dickhead's a dickhead, but he's one of the best there is. If they both come up with the same results, and really, when you look at the killer, he's just not . . ."

"Human? Bullshit. Bullshit. And one more bullshit. They're doing some sort of weird experiments in Rosenthall's lab. Something unauthorized and twisted."

"That's what I'm saying. They created a monster — a killer ape-man monster. And now it's broken out and wreaking havoc on the city. And —"

"Don't make me slap you. It's so damn girlie."

"Not when you're on the receiving end."

"Experiments," Eve continued. "The serum. It screws up the DNA, causes severe anemia. Louise said that could cause a green cast to the skin."

"All the way down?"

"Obviously."

"But the face, Dallas."

She wanted to believe it was prosthetics, a device, some sort of elaborate mask. But . . . "I don't know, but we're going to grill Rosenthall like a trout until he clears this up. Mr. Hyde," she muttered. "Maybe that's not so far off."

"Mr. Hyde?" Peabody scooted up and over in her seat. "Oh, oh, Rosenthall created the evil Dr. Jekyll. No wait, Dr. Jekyll's the good part. Hyde's the evil one. But they're the same person. Rosenthall's Mr. Hyde!"

"D minus, and only because you got the names right. Why would Rosenthall kill Jennifer Darnell — in that manner? That personal, intimate manner? The killer wanted her, and couldn't have her."

"Back to Pachai."

"Think about it. You said he loved her — and wit statements indicate she was interested. Now maybe he moved, she decided she wasn't interested after all. But who's the odd man out in this? Who got Darnell and her friend the jobs at Slice? Gets her and her friend work, but she's more interested in Gupta. And golly, where do we find one of the murder weapons? In Gupta's locker — with blood and brain matter still on it."

"Ken Dickerson. It is a frame-up."

"Gupta's Rosenthall's assistant. Dickerson's still an intern. Gupta's caught the eye of Darnell, even though Dickerson went to his uncle and got her work — then did her another favor and got work for Vix. Gupta comes from a family of doctors, scientists, and had a leg up since his father knows Rosenthall. Dickerson had to work his way through, push for scholarships. And Gupta's still ahead of him."

"Why not kill Pachai?"

"One of the first three vics got wind of something Dickerson was up to, so they had to go. What better way to destroy Gupta than by killing the girl he loved and pinning it on him? Whatever he's on makes him feel superior, but that was already in there. It makes him feel powerful, free. It makes him happy, and more, he's found out killing makes him even happier. He destroyed the lab, took the serum. He doesn't want anyone else to have what he's got. It's all his."

"It plays, but it doesn't explain the mutations."

"So Rosenthall better," she said as she pulled into the garage at Central. "We'll take him first."

CHAPTER
TEN

As Eve headed down to Homicide, Arianna sprang up from a bench in the corridor and rushed toward her. "Lieutenant Dallas, please, can you tell me what's happening? The police came to my home this morning. They said Eton's been murdered."

"That's correct."

"God. But when? How?"

"Shortly before one this morning, in Dr. Rosenthall's lab."

"In Justin's lab? But I don't . . ."

She closed her eyes a moment. "How can this be happening? They said we needed to come here — Justin and I. They took him somewhere else, wouldn't let me stay with him. They just said I had to wait. It's been more than an hour."

"I'm sorry it's taken so long. I'm going to be talking to Dr. Rosenthall shortly."

"But what happened? My God, this is a nightmare. Eton murdered, and in Justin's lab."

"Do you know why Dr. Billingsly would have been in Dr. Rosenthall's lab at that time of night?"

"No. No. He shouldn't have been. He's not involved in Justin's work. The killer must have been after Justin.

After Justin." Arianna rubbed a hand between her breasts back and forth. "He was going to work late, stay in his office again last night, but I asked him not to. I asked him to come home with me, stay with me. I wanted him with me, and I was upset enough that he gave in."

"You left the Center together?"

"Yes, about eleven thirty, I think. I had a fundraiser, and called Justin from the car when I left."

"Did anyone stay in the lab?"

"I don't know. Justin met me out front. We were together all night. I swear it. You can't believe Justin had anything to do with this. I know people talk about Eton being jealous of him."

"Was he?"

"Yes, but Justin isn't bothered by it. We — God, it seems cruel now — we'd joke about it sometimes. Can I see him now? Do we need a lawyer?"

"He's not under arrest, but I need to ask him a few questions. If he wants a lawyer present he can have one. Peabody, why don't you take Ms. Whitwood to the lounge? She can wait there while we talk to Dr. Rosenthall. It shouldn't be long."

As long as it takes, Eve thought as she headed toward the first interview room.

Justin straightened in his chair when Eve entered.

"So it's true," he said, "about Billingsly. He's dead."

"Yes. Record on, Dallas, Lieutenant Eve, in Interview with Dr. Justin Rosenthall on the matters of Darnell, Vix, and Bickford, case number H-45893, and

116

Eton Billingsly, case number H-43898. I have to record this. Procedure."

"I understand."

"I'm also going to read you your rights." As she did, Justin said nothing. "Do you understand your rights and obligations?"

"Yes. You think I killed them?"

She let the question hang a moment. He looked worn-out, she noted, as Arianna had.

"All the victims were connected to you and the Center. Billingsly was murdered in your lab."

"In *my* lab?"

"Yes. There are questions that have to be asked, but first, I'd like a sample of your DNA."

"My — all right, but it's on file."

"Just consider it a spot check." She took out a swab.

When it was done, she went to the door, passed it off to the waiting uniform.

She sat at the table across from Justin. "What was Billingsly doing in your lab?"

"I have no idea. He shouldn't have been there. He shouldn't have been able to get in without my authorization. How did he?"

"He cloned your swipe card and had a recording of your voice."

Justin simply stared at her. "He went that far? He disliked me — that's not news — but I can't believe he'd go as far as breaking into the lab. And for what?"

"Would he have business with your assistant or interns?"

"No, none I can think of. And he knew none of us were there. I saw him before I left, and he commented on the fact that I was actually going home."

"You didn't get along."

"Not well." Justin braced his elbows on the table, pushed his hands over his face, back into his hair. "That's no secret, as he made it very clear he didn't think I was good enough for Ari — and he was."

"That must have pissed you off."

"Some," he admitted. "But frankly, I didn't give Billingsly much thought. Arianna loves me; we're about to be married. And my work occupies the rest of my thoughts at this stage."

"What is this stage?"

"We're about to begin the next round of testing."

"Meaning?" Eve said as Peabody entered. "Peabody, Detective Delia, entering Interview. Go on, Doctor."

"We've injected a test group of lab rats with specific addictive substances over a course of time."

"You've made addicts out of rats?"

"Yes. We observe and monitor, chart, record. Now we'll inject them with the serum, run them through tests. Once we —"

"You don't test on human subjects."

"No. That's months off, maybe years. This isn't a quick process. We can't risk testing an unproven substance on a human being."

"It must be tempting to push it some, to kick up the pace."

"You don't go into research to rush."

"Do your assistants ever get antsy?"

118

"I'm sorry?"

"Maybe your assistants want to take it up a notch, show off some, impress you."

"They're young. Sure, there's some frustration, impatience — competition from time to time. But we have a very strict protocol, a timetable, procedures that must be followed not only for success but for safety."

"Who has access to the serum?"

"It's locked in the lab, in an environmentally controlled case. No one but myself and Pachai have access. You don't think Billingsly tried to —"

"The case was open," Eve told him. "And empty."

"Empty?" Looking stricken, Rosenthall rubbed at his temple. "The serum's gone? God. *God!* We're so close. A competing lab? Espionage? Would Billingsly have done that?"

"Your two interns can't access the serum?"

"No. Well, that's not completely accurate. Ken's worked late with me several nights, and I gave him the code. I change it every three days. I'd have changed it this morning, in fact. We can re-create the serum. But the time lost . . ." He shook his head. "But I don't understand what this has to do with the murders, with Jen and the boys. I can't believe they'd be involved in some plot to steal or sell the work."

"That's okay. I understand. Interview end. If you'd just wait here a minute. Peabody?"

"You're cutting him loose?" Peabody asked when they stepped out.

"I want you to take him to the lounge, ask him and Arianna to wait. I might need him to talk to Dickerson, interpret some of the science stuff when we get to it. Then do a round with Gupta. He may have something to add here, and he knows you now."

"Okay. You're taking Dickerson alone?"

"I'll start on him. When you think you've got all you can get from Gupta, take him to the lounge, then come in to Interview."

"Check."

"And bring Dickerson a drink."

Peabody sighed. "Because I'm good cop."

"So far." Eve walked down to the next interview room, entered.

"Dallas, Lieutenant Eve," she began and completed the documentation. "Hey, Ken, you look a little wrung out."

"I've been waiting a long time. Like two hours."

A little sweaty, Eve observed. Hollow-eyed and very pale. "These things take time." She read him his rights, watched those hollow eyes widen.

"I'm a suspect? Why are you saying all that?"

"For your protection, Ken. Just procedure. You know about procedure. Do you understand your rights, your obligations?"

"Yes, but I don't understand why —"

"Four people are dead, Ken, and you knew all of them."

"I'm not the only one who —"

"We're talking to the others. So what did you think of Billingsly?" she continued, conversationally. "An asshole, right?"

120

"I don't really have an opinion. I didn't know him, really."

"Take my word. Asshole. Anybody who tries to horn in on another man's woman, especially when she's not interested, is an asshole."

She smiled when she said it, watched his eyes skitter away. "I nearly forgot." She took out a swab. "I need some spit. DNA check."

"I — I don't have to do that."

"Seriously? It's just some spit, Ken."

"I don't have to do that unless you have a warrant. That's my right."

"Suit yourself." She shrugged. "Now, about assholes."

"Should I get a lawyer?"

"Do you want one? Fine with me. It'll take more time. Probably a couple more hours." She started to rise.

"It's okay, for now. I just want to get out of here."

"Can't blame you. Like I said, you look wrung out. Up late?"

"I didn't sleep well. It's hard, with what happened."

"I bet. You liked Jen."

"Everybody liked Jen."

"But you really liked her. You got her a job."

"It was no big deal."

"Come on, take some credit. An addict with barely a month's recovery under her belt before you asked your uncle to give her a break. Then you do her another solid and help her addict friend get a job. She owed you."

"I was just trying to help."

"Did she pay you back?"

"I don't know what you mean."

"I don't think she did, not when she had her eye on Pachai — and he had his on her. That must've stung."

He scratched at his arms as if something crawled along his skin. "She was just a friend."

"Because that's the way she wanted it. And Pachai, what did he do for her? He didn't get her and her addict friend jobs. His uncle didn't give her food to take home. He comes from money, though. Isn't that always the way? Gets to be Rosenthall's head guy — over you. You worked harder, I bet. Put in more hours. You're smarter — I can tell. You've got ideas, don't you, Ken? Ideas about the serum."

She leaned forward. No visible scratches, she thought. But he'd left his hair down, over the back of his neck.

"I bet you put in lots of your own time on that project. Off the books, so to speak. Busting your ass. Rosenthall's so conservative, such a stickler for protocol, procedure. But you've got balls. You're willing to take some risks. Did Jen find out you were taking one?"

He kept scratching, swallowing, looking anywhere but at Eve. "I don't know what you're talking about."

"She came in the lab a lot, didn't she? Making excuses to drop in so she could see Pachai. Flirted with him right in front of you. Did she come by when you were working alone one night? Off the books. Did you let her in?"

"We're not allowed to work in the lab off hours unless Dr. Rosenthall's there."

122

"Rules." Eve waved them away. "Real innovation says screw the rules. Real progress is risky, takes gambles. And Rosenthall's poking along with his yes-man Gupta getting all the attention — and the girl. It's not right. But you can show them you're better, smarter. Did she catch you at it, or did you tell her? Had to brag about it. But she still didn't want you. In fact, she threatened to tell on you if you didn't stop. To tell Rosenthall you were experimenting with his work, testing it, and not on rats."

He began to shiver now, as if cold even while the sweat dribbled down his temples. "You're making all this up."

"Am I? Scientists keep records. We're going to get a search warrant for your apartment, and we're going to find yours. We're going to find the pipe you used to beat Coby Vix to death with. Then —"

"You can't find the pipe at my place because . . ."

"Why is that, Ken?"

"I'm not talking anymore."

"Suit yourself." Eve sat back, watched him sweat a few moments until Peabody came in with a tube of ginger ale.

"Peabody, Detective Delia, entering Interview. He could use that. Have a drink, Ken, take a little time to think. The way I look at it, things just got out of hand, out of your control. You had a really bad reaction to the serum."

"I'm not saying anything else." But he took the tube, cracked it, guzzled.

And when she came back in, Eve thought, she'd take the tube — and have his DNA.

"Think about it," Eve suggested. "Interview pause. Dallas, Lieutenant Eve, and Peabody, Detective Delia, exiting the room."

"He looks sweaty, shaky," Peabody began outside the door. "He looks like —"

"An addict jonesing for a fix. He's scared, too. He's either going to crack or lawyer up — that could go either way. Let's get a search warrant for his apartment. We've got enough for that. He's got logs and records. That stupid cape, the gloves, the shoes, maybe the knife and scalpel."

"Maybe we should have Rosenthall observe the next round. Like you said, if he gets into the science, Rosenthall could tell us what it means."

"Good idea. Go get him, take him to an observation room. I'm going to give Dickerson another couple minutes."

She could use a drink herself, Eve thought, and gave Vending a hard eye. The machines didn't always cooperate with her.

"Let me do that." Roarke plugged in credits, ordered her a tube of Pepsi.

"Thanks. Come to watch the show?"

"It's usually worth the price of admission."

"I've got Dickerson sweating in the box. Literally. I think he's been taking the serum — or a version of it. And I think he dosed himself real good two nights in a row. It's got him strung out. I'm about to go in for the second round. Peabody's bringing Rosenthall into

124

Observation, in case we need an interpreter for the science."

"I'll go find them."

He gave her a tap on the chin, then strolled off — as at home in the cop shop as she was, she thought.

She cracked the tube, took a long drink, then walked back to the interview room. When she stepped in, Dickerson was standing in the far corner, facing the wall. His shoulders shook.

"Dallas, Lieutenant Eve, reentering Interview. Jesus, Ken, man up."

"That's Dr. Chaos to you."

She arched her eyebrows at the rough sound of his voice. "Now we're getting somewhere. Have a seat, Doc, and we'll —"

He turned. She'd thought little could genuinely surprise her at this stage of her life and career, but she froze in shock.

His face rippled in front of her eyes. Sickly green, it twisted itself until the jaw locked at a grotesque angle. His teeth sharpened; his eyes protruded and bulged in their sockets, and began to gleam red.

"And I'm not a man."

She heard the snap and crack of migrating bones as his spine seemed to warp. "I'm a god."

She pulled her weapon. "What you are is under arrest."

He leaped at her. She got a stream off, was sure she struck midbody, but he was so *fast*. She had a fraction of a second to prepare, and used the force of his body

125

ramming hers to go down, kick up, and send him flying over her and into the wall.

He careened off, bloodied, and nimble as a spider. This time when she fired, he jerked. Then he smiled.

"Oooh, it tickles! I'm so much stronger now."

"So I see. But not pretty. You're smart." He would attack again, she thought. There was too much animal in him not to. "You're in the middle of Cop Central. Even if you get through me, you won't get out. You'll die here."

"I can't die. But you can. You're an insect to me. All of you. Weak and breakable."

"He's still in you. The weak and breakable Dickerson."

"Not for much longer. He cried over the girl, but he enjoyed killing Billingsly. He'll enjoy killing you. We're going to carve out your heart, and eat it."

She fired again, kept firing. It slowed him, caused him to stumble, but he came on.

The door burst open. Roarke rushed in, steps ahead of Peabody and a swarm of cops. Chaos whirled, snarled — jittered from the stun streams.

"Go down, you fuck!" Eve shouted.

"Allow me." Face cold and fierce, Roarke rammed his fists into the twisted face. Right, left, right again.

Blood streaming, body spasming, Chaos went down.

"Jesus Christ, Jesus Christ, Jesus Christ." Eve muttered the oaths — prayers — as she snapped on restraints. "I want leg irons," she called out. "Now. Peabody, keep your weapon on him."

"Believe me," her partner responded.

"I want him shackled, in a cage, before he comes to. Isolation. Let's move!"

"Are you hurt?" Roarke gripped her hand as she rose.

"No. I've got to get him contained. I'll be back. And hey, thanks for the assist," she added as she moved aside to let some of the men lift Chaos.

Roarke watched her go, then glanced down at his raw knuckles. "Ah, well."

Epilogue

Eve found him waiting in her office, settled in her ratty visitor's chair with his PPC. He set it aside when she came in, and with one look at her face, went to the AutoChef, programmed coffee for both of them.

"He's dying." Eve dropped down at her desk. "Multiple organ failure — Louise had that one. And he's got a brain tumor for good measure. They're not going to be able to save him."

"I'm trying to be sorry, as you seem to be."

"He was an idiot — Dickerson. Jealous, ambitious, reckless. But he wasn't a murderer. Or not until he started taking the serum. His version of it. He'd improved it, so he thought. He was going to impress the girl, his boss, the whole fucking world. Now he's dying because he unleashed something in himself that perverted what he was, what he wanted. Something he couldn't control."

Roarke sat on the corner of her desk, facing her. "He would have killed you."

"Yeah. What he became was as addicted to killing as Dickerson was to the serum. As the people Rosenthall's trying to help are to the illegals. Rosenthall's with him now — pretty much crushed. Dickerson's barely able to talk, but we got all we need to close the cases."

"It's never just about closed cases for you."

"Four people slaughtered. And now we'll have five bodies. Dickerson was dead the first time he took the serum. He just didn't know it. He asked Darnell to come into the lab. He was so proud, had to show off. Had to hope she'd see how special he was, and want him the way he wanted her. Instead, she disapproved, told him he had to go to Rosenthall, had to stop."

"She would have recognized the addiction," Roarke concluded.

"Yeah, I'd say. She was black-and-white on it. If he didn't tell his boss, she would, because he was making himself sick, she said."

"And that only made him take more."

"He promised he'd do what she said, then increased the dose. To prove to her he was better than Pachai, better even than Rosenthall."

"And Chaos was born."

"I guess that's true enough. He says he thought the murders were a dream, a hallucination."

"You don't believe that."

"No," she confirmed. "I don't. He knew what he'd done. He just couldn't face it on one side, couldn't give it up on the other. Dickerson told us Billingsly was trying to hack into Rosenthall's computer when he got to the lab."

"Jealousy again."

"The green-skinned monster."

Roarke started to correct her, then shrugged. "Well, in this case."

"And this case is closed." She finished off her coffee, set it and the sadness aside. "I need to write it up, and I promised Nadine I'd give her a head start. I don't know why."

"Friendship, and because you know she'll be fair and accurate. I'll leave you to it then, find myself a spot to finish a bit of business. Tag me when you're done. We missed breakfast altogether. I'll take you to lunch — whenever."

"I can grab something. You don't have to wait around."

"Eve." He touched the shaggy tips of her hair. "I'd just stepped into Observation when he turned around. I saw what he was, or what he was becoming. We never quite see everything there is, do we? What I did see was the delight — the murderous delight on his face. I didn't know if I'd get there, get to you, in time."

"I'd stunned the shit out of him," she began. "And yeah, he might've gotten a piece of me anyway. You finished him off real nice."

"Well then, you'd loosened the lid. I'll wait for you." He leaned forward, touched his lips to hers. "Always."

"Sap."

"Guilty. And when we get home tonight, we'll take care of that arm."

"I know what *that* means."

He laughed, kissed her again. "You've had it cradled since you sat down."

130

She glanced down, saw he was right. "I guess it took a knock in there." She released it, took his hand to examine his knuckles. "You, too."

"Then we'll take care of each other."

"Sounds good."

And it did, she thought, when he'd left her to find his quiet spot. Before the work, she rose, walked to her skinny window. She looked out at New York — safe, for the moment, from one of the monsters who hunted.

And stood awhile, holding vigil for the dying.

POSSESSION
IN DEATH

Love is strong as death.
                    SONG OF SOLOMON

Whence and what art thou, execrable
shape?
                    JOHN MILTON

CHAPTER
ONE

She spent the morning with a murderer.

He'd been under guard in a hospital bed recovering from a near-fatal wound — courtesy of a misstep by his partner in crime — but she'd had no sympathy.

She was glad he'd lived, wished him a long, long life — in an off-planet concrete cage. She believed the case she and her team had built to be solid — as did the nearly gleeful prosecuting attorney. The sprinkles on the icing of this particular cupcake was the confession she'd finessed out of him as he'd sneered at her.

Given that he'd tried to kill her less than twenty-four hours before, the sneer was small change.

Sylvester Moriarity would receive the best medical care New York could provide, then he'd join his friend Winston Dudley behind bars until what promised to be a sensational, media-soaked trial, given their family fortunes and names.

Case closed, she told herself as she pushed her way through the heat-soaked Saturday afternoon traffic toward home. The dead now had the only justice she could offer, and their families and friends the comfort — if comfort it was — that those responsible would pay.

But it haunted her: the waste, the cruelty, the utter selfishness of two men who were so puffed up by their own importance, their *station*, that they'd considered murder a form of entertainment, a twisted sort of indulgence.

She manuevered through New York traffic, barely hearing the blasts of horns, the annoyingly cheerful hype of the ad blimps heralding midsummer sales at the Sky Mall. Tourists swarmed the city — and likely the Sky Mall as well — chowing down on soy dogs from the smoking glide-carts, looking for souvies and bargains among the shops and street vendors.

A boiling stew, she thought, in the heat and humidity of summer 2060.

She caught the lightning move of a nimble-fingered street thief, bumping through a couple of tourists more intent on gawking at the buildings and their ringing people glides than their own security. He had the wallet in the goody slit of his baggy cargos in half a finger snap and slithered like a snake through the forest of people lumbering across the crosswalk.

If she'd been on foot, or at least headed in the same direction, she'd have pursued — and the chase might've lifted her mood. But he and his booty smoked away, and he'd no doubt continue to score well on today's target shoot.

Life went on.

When Lieutenant Eve Dallas finally drove through the stately gates of home, she reminded herself of that again. Life went on — and in her case, today, that included a cookout, a horde of cops, and her odd assortment of friends. A couple years before, it would've been the last way she'd have spent a Saturday, but things had changed.

Her living arrangements certainly had, from a sparsely furnished apartment to the palace-fortress Roarke had built. Her husband — and *that* was a change, even if they'd just celebrated their second year of marriage — had the vision, the need, and, God knew, the means to create the gorgeous home with its myriad rooms filled with style and function. Here the grass was rich summer green, the trees and flowers plentiful.

Here was peace and warmth and welcome. And she needed them, maybe just a little desperately at the moment.

She left her vehicle at the front entrance, knowing Summerset, Roarke's majordomo, would send it to its place in the garage. And hoped, just this once, he wasn't looming like a scarecrow in the foyer.

She wanted the cool and quiet of the bedroom she shared with Roarke, a few minutes of solitude. Time, she thought as she strode toward the doors, to shake off this mood before the invasion.

Halfway to the doors, she stopped. The front wasn't the only way in, for Christ's sake — and why hadn't she ever thought of that before? On impulse, she jogged around — long legs eating up ground — crossed one of the patios, turned through a small, walled garden, and went in through a side door. Into a parlor or sitting room or morning room — who knew? she thought with a roll of tired brown eyes — and made her way as sneakily as the street thief across the hallway, down and into the more familiar territory of the game room, where she knew the lay of the land.

She called the elevator and considered it a small, personal victory when the doors shut her in. "Master bedroom," she ordered, then just leaned back against the wall, shut her eyes, while the unit navigated its way.

When she stepped into the bedroom, she raked a hand through her messy cap of brown hair, stripped the jacket off her lanky frame, and tossed it at the handiest chair. She stepped onto the platform and sat on the side of the lake-sized bed. If she'd believed she could escape into sleep, she'd have stretched out, but there was too much in her head, in her belly, for rest.

So she simply sat, veteran cop, Homicide lieutenant who'd walked through blood and death more times than she could count, and mourned a little.

Roarke found her there.

He could gauge her state of mind by the slump of her shoulders, by the way she sat, staring out the window. He walked to her, sat beside her, took her hand.

"I should've gone with you."

She shook her head but leaned against him. "No place for civilians in Interview, and nothing you could've done anyway if I'd stretched it and brought you in as expert consultant. I had him cold and cut through his battalion of expensive lawyers like a fucking machete. I thought the PA was going to kiss me on the mouth."

140

He brought the hand he held to his lips. "And still you're sad."

She closed her eyes, comforted a little by the solidity of him beside her, by that whisper of Ireland in his voice, even by the scent so uniquely him. "Not sad, or . . . I don't know what the hell I am. I should be buzzed. I did the job; I slammed it shut — and I got to look them both in the face and let them know it."

She shoved up, paced to the window, away again, and realized it wasn't peace and comfort she wanted after all. Not quite yet. It was a place to let it go, let it out, spew the rage.

"He was pissed. Moriarity. Lying there with that hole in his chest his pal put into him with his freaking antique Italian foil."

"The one meant for you," Roarke reminded her.

"Yeah. And he's pissed, seriously pissed, Dudley missed and it wasn't me on a slab at the morgue."

"I expect he was," Roarke said coolly. "But that's not what's got you going."

She paused a minute, just looked at him. Stunning blue eyes in a stunning face, the mane of thick black hair, that poet's mouth set firm now because she'd made him think of her on that slab at the morgue.

"You know they never had a chance to take me. You were there."

"And still he drew blood, didn't he?" Roarke nodded at the healing wound on her arm.

She tapped it. "And this helped sew them up. Attempted murder of a police officer just trowels on the icing. They didn't make their next score. Now they have to end their competition with a tie, which oddly enough is what I think they always wanted. They just planned for the contest to go on a lot longer. And you know what the prize was at the end? Do you know what the purse for this goddamn tournament was?"

"I don't, no, but I see you got it out of Moriarity today."

"Yeah, I wound him up so tight he had to let it spring out. A dollar. A fucking dollar, Roarke — just one big joke between them. And it makes me sick."

It shocked, even appalled her a little, that her eyes stung, that she felt tears pressing hard. "It makes me sick," she repeated. "All those people dead, all those lives broken and shattered, and *this* makes me sick? I don't know why, I just don't know why it churns my stomach. I've seen worse. God, we've both seen worse."

"But rarely more futile." He stood, took her arms, gently rubbing. "No reason, no mad vendetta or fevered dream, no vengeance or greed or fury. Just a cruel game. Why shouldn't it make you sick? It does me as well."

"I contacted the next of kin," she began. "Even the ones we found from before they started this matchup in New York. That's why I'm late getting back. I thought I needed to, and thought if I closed it all the way, I'd feel better. I got gratitude. I got anger and tears, everything you expect. And every one of them asked me why. Why had these men killed their daughter, their husband, their mother?"

"And what did you tell them?"

142

"Sometimes there's no why, or not one we can understand." She squeezed her eyes tight. "I want to be pissed."

"You are, under it. And under that, you know you did good work. And you're alive, darling Eve." He drew her in to kiss her brow. "Which, to take this to their level, makes them losers."

"I guess it does. I guess that's going to have to be enough."

She took his face in her hands, smiled a little. "And there's the added bonus that they hate us both. Really hate us. That adds a boost."

"I can't think of anyone I'd rather be hated by, or anyone I'd rather be hated with."

Now the smile moved into her eyes. "Me either. If I keep that front and center, I could be in the mood to party. I guess we should go down and do whatever we're supposed to do before everybody gets here."

"Change first. You'll feel more in the party mode without your boots and weapon."

By the time she'd changed trousers for cotton pants, boots for skids, and made it downstairs, she heard voices in the foyer. She spotted her partner, Peabody, her short, dark ponytail bouncing, summery dress swirling. Peabody's cohab, e-detective and premier geek McNab, stood beside her in a skin tank crisscrossed with more colors than an atomic rainbow paired with baggy, hot pink knee shorts and gel flips.

He turned, the forest of silver rings on his left earlobe shimmering, and shot Eve a wide grin. "Hey, Dallas. We brought you something."

"My granny's homemade wine." Peabody held up the bottle. "I know you've got a wine cellar the size of California, but we thought you'd get a charge. It's good stuff."

"Let's go out and open it up. I'm ready for some good stuff."

Peabody kept eye contact, quirked her brows. "All okay?"

"The PA's probably still doing his happy dance. Case closed," she said, and left out the rest. No point in adding the details now that would leave her partner as troubled as she'd been.

"We'll have the first drink with a toast to the NYPSD's Homicide — and Electronic Detectives divisions," Roarke said with a wink for McNab.

The wide stone terrace held tables already loaded with food and shaded by umbrellas, and the gardens exploded with color and scent. The monster grill Roarke had conquered — mostly — looked formidable, and the wine was indeed good stuff.

Within thirty minutes, the scent of grilling meat mixed with the perfume of summer flowers. The terrace, the chairs around the tables, the gardens filled with people. It still amazed her she'd somehow collected so many.

Her cops — everyone who'd worked the Dudley-Moriarity case — along with Cher Reo, the ADA, newlyweds Dr. Louise DiMatto and retired licensed companion Charles Monroe stood, sat, lounged, or stuffed their faces.

144

Morris, the ME who'd inspired the impulse for her to arrange this shindig to help with his lingering grief over his murdered love, shared a brew with Father Lopez, who'd become his friend and counselor.

Sort of weird having a priest at a party — even one she liked and respected — but at least he wasn't wearing the getup.

Nadine Furst, bestselling author and ace reporter, chatted happily with Dr. Mira, department shrink, and Mira's adorable husband, Dennis.

It was good, she decided, to blow off steam this way, to gather together to do it, even if gathering together wasn't as natural for her as for some. It was good to watch Feeney kibitz Roarke's grill technique, and watch Trueheart show off his pretty, shy-eyed girlfriend.

Hell, she might just have another glass of Granny Peabody's wine and —

The thought winged away when she heard the bright laugh.

Mavis Freestone rushed out on silver sandals that laced past the hem of her flippy, thigh-baring lavender skirt. Her hair, perched in a crowning tail, matched the skirt. In her arms she carried baby Bella. Leonardo, beaming at his girls, followed.

"Dallas!"

"I thought you were in London," Eve said when she was enveloped in color and scent and joy.

"We couldn't miss a party! We'll go back tomorrow. Trina stopped off to talk to Summerset."

Eve felt her skin chill. "Trina . . ."

"Don't worry, she's here to party, not to give you a treatment. She did Bella's hair — isn't it mag?"

A half a zillion sunny curls surrounded the baby's happy face. Every single one bounced with tiny pink bows.

"Yeah, it's —"

"Oh, everybody who counts is here! I've got to give out squeezes. Here, hold Bellamisa a minute."

"I'll get us a drink." Leonardo patted Eve's head with his huge hand, then glided away in his calf-baring red crops.

"I —" As Eve's arms were immediately loaded with bouncing, gooing baby, the protest ended on a strangled gulp.

"Got some weight to you these days," Eve managed, then scanned the crowd for a sucker to pass the load to. Bella squealed, sending Eve's heart rate soaring, then grabbed a fistful of Eve's hair, tugged with surprising force.

And planted a wet, openmouthed kiss on Eve's cheek. "Slooch!" said Bella.

"What does that mean? Oh God."

"Smooch," Mavis called out, gesturing with a frothy pink drink. "She wants you to kiss her back."

"Man. Okay, fine." Gingerly, Eve pecked her lips at Bella's cheek.

Obviously pleased, Bella let out a laugh so like Mavis's, Eve grinned. "Okay, kid, let's go find someone else for you to slooch."

CHAPTER
TWO

Nobody ate like cops. Priests didn't do half bad, Eve observed, and doctors held their own, she decided as Louise, Morris, and Mira chowed down on burgers. But against a horde of cops, a ravaging pack of hyenas would fall short.

Maybe it was all the missed meals, the clichéd donut grabbed on the fly. But when cops sat down to free food, they did so with single-minded focus.

"This is nice." Nadine stepped over, tapped her wineglass to Eve's beer bottle. "A nice day, a nice group, a nice chance to just relax and hang. Which is why I'm waiting until Monday to nag you into coming on *Now* to discuss the Dudley-Moriarity murders."

"It's wrapped."

"I know it's wrapped — I have my sources. If I hadn't been out of town doing publicity for the book, I'd have been in your face before this."

Nadine smiled. She wore her sun-streaked hair longer and looser and had chosen a sleeveless, floating tank over pants cropped short to show off an ankle chain — but the camera-ready reporter was still in there.

"But I'll stay out of it today," Nadine added, and took another sip of wine. "You know what I like when you have one of these gatherings, Dallas?"

"The food and alcohol?"

"It's always first-rate, but beyond that. It's always such an interesting mix of people. I know I can sit down next to anyone here and not be bored. You've got a talent for collecting the diverse and the interesting. I was just talking with Crack," she added, referring to the six and a half foot, tattooed sex club owner. "Now I think I'm going to sit down next to the shy and strapping Officer Trueheart and the pretty young thing he's with."

"Cassie from Records."

"Cassie from Records," Nadine repeated. "I think I'd like to find out just what's going on between those two."

Eve wandered toward the grill, where Roarke had passed the torch to Feeney, under the supervision of Dennis Mira. They were sort of an odd pair — diverse, as Nadine had said — the lanky, dreamy-eyed professor and the rumpled cop with his explosion of ginger hair.

"How's it going?" she asked.

"Got another couple orders for cow burgers, and these kabob deals." Feeney flipped a patty.

"I don't know where they put it." Dennis shook his head.

"Cop stomachs." Feeney winked at Eve. "We eat what's in front of us, and plenty of it when we get the chance."

"Somebody ought to save room for lemon meringue pie and strawberry shortcake."

Feeney stopped with a burger on his flipper. "We got lemon meringue pie and strawberry shortcake?"

"That's the word on the street."

"Where's it at?"

"I don't know. Ask Summerset."

"Don't think I won't." He flipped the burger then shoved the spatula at Dennis. "Take over. I'm getting my share before these vultures get wind."

As Feeney rushed off, Dennis's eyes went even softer. "Is there whipped cream?"

"Probably."

"Ah." He handed her the spatula. "Would you mind?" he asked, adding a fatherly pat on the head. "I have a weakness for shortcake and whipped cream."

"Um —" But he was already strolling off.

Eve looked down at the sizzling patties, the skewered vegetables. It wasn't quite as terrifying as having a drooling baby dumped in her arms, but . . . How the hell did you know when they were done? Did something signal? Should she poke at them or leave them alone?

Everything sizzled and smoked, and there were countless dials and gauges. When she cautiously lifted another shiny lid, she found fat dogs — probably actual pig meat — cooking away like hot, engorged penises.

She closed the lid again, then let out a huff of relief when Roarke joined her.

"They deserted the field, seduced by rumors of cake and pie. You handle this." She surrendered the spatula.

"I might do something that puts Louise and her doctor's bag to work."

He looked at the sizzle and smoke as she'd often seen him look at some thorny computer code. With the light of challenge in his eyes.

"It's actually satisfying, the grilling business." He offered the spatula. "I could teach you."

"No thanks. Eating it's satisfying, and I've already done that."

He slid the burgers from grill to platter, then used some sort of tongs to transfer the kabobs.

"If I'd known they were done, I could've done that."

"You have other talents." He leaned down, the platter of food between them, and kissed her.

A good moment, she thought — the scents, the voices, the hot summer sun. Eve started to smile, then saw Lopez crossing in their direction. He walked like the boxer he'd been, she thought, the compact body light on the feet.

"Ready for another round, Chale?" Roarke asked him.

"The first was more than enough. I want to thank you both for having me. You have a beautiful home, beautiful friends."

"You're not leaving already?"

"I'm afraid I have to. I have the evening Mass, with a baptism. The family requested me, so I have to get back to St. Cristóbal's and prepare. But I can't think of a nicer way to have spent the afternoon."

"I'll drive you," Eve said.

150

"That's kind of you." He looked at her — warm brown eyes that to her mind always held a lingering hint of sadness. "But I couldn't take you away from your guests."

"No problem. They're focused on food, and dessert's coming up."

He continued to look at her, to search, and she knew he saw something as he nodded. "I'd appreciate it."

"Why don't you take this?" Roarke handed Eve the platter. "Set it out, and I'll have Summerset box up some of the desserts for Chale."

"You'd make me a hero in the rectory tonight. I'll just say my good-byes then."

"Thanks," Eve said when Lopez moved back to the party. "There's just a couple of things I wanted his take on. It won't take long."

"Go ahead then. I'll have your vehicle brought around."

She wasn't sure how to approach it, or even why she felt the need to. But he made it easy for her — maybe that's what men like Lopez did.

"You want to ask me about Li," he began as she passed through the gates.

"Yeah, for one thing. I see Morris mostly over dead bodies, but I can get a sense of where he is. Just by wardrobe for a start. I know he's coming through it, but . . ."

"It's hard to watch a friend grieve. I can't tell you specifics, as some of what we've talked about was in confidence. He's a strong and spiritual man, one who — like you — lives with death."

"It helps — the work. I can see it," Eve said, "and he's said it does."

"Yes, tending to those whose lives have been taken, like his Amaryllis. It centers him. He misses her, misses the potential of what they might have made together. I can tell you most of his anger has passed. It's a start."

"I don't know how people get rid of the anger. I don't know if I'd want to in his place."

"You gave him justice — earthly justice. From there he needed to find acceptance, and then the faith that Amaryllis is in the hands of God. Or, if not God, the belief that she, too, has moved on to the next phase."

"If the next phase is so great, why do we work so hard to stay in this one? Why does death seem so *useless* and hurt so damn much? All those people, just going along, living their lives, until somebody decides to end it for them. We should be pissed off. The dead should be pissed off. Maybe they are, because sometimes they just won't let go."

"Murder breaks both God's law and man's, and it requires — demands — punishment."

"So I put them in a cage and the next stop is a fiery hell? Maybe. I don't know. But what about the murdered? Some of them are innocent, just living their lives. But others? Others are as bad, or nearly, as the one who ended them. In this phase, I have to treat them all the same, do the job, close the case. I can do that. I have to do that. But maybe I wonder, sometimes, if it's enough for the innocent, and for the ones — like Morris — who get left behind."

"You've had a difficult week," he murmured.

152

"And then some."

"If closing cases was all that mattered to you, if it began and ended there, you would never have suggested your friend meet with me. You and I wouldn't be having this conversation. And you wouldn't, couldn't, maintain your passion for the work I believe you were born to do."

"Sometimes I wish I could see, or feel . . . No, I wish I could know, even once, that it's enough."

He reached out, touched her hand briefly. "Our work isn't the same, but some of the questions we ask ourselves are."

She glanced at him. Out of the side window she caught the movement. For a moment it seemed the streets, the sidewalks, were empty. Except for the old woman who staggered, who lifted an already bloodied hand to her chest an instant before she tumbled off the curb and into the street.

Eve slammed the brakes, flicked on her flashers. Even as she leaped out of the car, she yanked her 'link from her pocket. "Emergency sequence, Dallas, Lieutenant Eve. I need MTs, I need a bus, six hundred block of 120 Street. First aid kit in the trunk," she shouted at Lopez. "Code's two-five-six-zero-Baker-Zulu. Female victim," she continued, dropping down beside the woman. "Multiple stab wounds. Hold on," she muttered. "Hold on." And dropping the 'link, she pressed her hands to the chest wound. "Help's coming."

"Beata." The woman's eyelids flickered, opened to reveal eyes so dark Eve could barely gauge the pupils. "Trapped. The red door. Help her."

"Help's coming. Give me your name," Eve said as Lopez pulled padding from the first aid kit. "What's your name?"

"She is Beata. My beauty. She can't get out."

"Who did this to you?"

"He is the devil." Those black eyes bore into Eve's. The words she pushed out held an accent thick as the heat.

Eastern European, Eve thought, filing it in her mind.

"You . . . you are the warrior. Find Beata. Save Beata."

"Okay. Don't worry." Eve glanced at Lopez, who shook his head. He began to murmur in Latin as he crossed himself and made the sign on the woman's forehead.

"The devil killed my body. I cannot fight, I cannot find. I cannot free her. You must. You are the one. We speak to the dead."

Eve heard the sirens, knew they would be too late. The pads, her own hands, the street was soaked with blood. "Okay. Don't worry about her. I'll find her. Tell me your name."

"I am Gizi. I am the promise. You must let me in and keep your promise."

"Okay, okay. Don't worry. I'll take care of it." Hurry, her mind shouted at the sirens. For God's sake, hurry.

"My blood, your blood." The woman gripped the hand Eve pressed to her chest wound with surprising strength, scoring the flesh with her fingernails. "My heart, your heart. My soul, your soul. Take me in."

Eve ignored the quick pain from the little cuts in her palm. "Sure. All right. Here they come." She looked up as the ambulance screamed around the corner, then back into those fierce, depthless black eyes.

Something burned in her hand, up her arm, until the shocking blow to her chest stole her breath. The light flashed, blinding her, then went to utter dark.

In the dark were voices and deeper shadows and the bright form of a young woman — slim in build, a waterfall of black hair and eyes of deep, velvet brown.

She is Beata. I am the promise, and the promise is in you. You are the warrior, and the warrior holds me. We are together until the promise is kept and the fight is done.

"Eve. Eve. Lieutenant Dallas!"

She jerked, sucked in air like a diver surfacing, and found herself staring at Lopez's face. "What?"

"Thank God. You're all right?"

"Yeah." She raked a bloodied hand through her hair. "What the hell happened?"

"I honestly don't know." He glanced over to where, a foot away, two MTs worked on the woman. "She's gone. There was a light — such a light. I've never seen . . . Then she was gone, and you were . . ." He struggled for words. "Not unconscious, but blank. Just not there for a moment. I had to pull you away so they could get to her. You saw the light?"

"I saw something." Felt something, she thought. Heard something.

Now she saw only an old woman whose blood stained the street. "I have to call this in. I think you're going to be late for Mass. I need you to give a statement."

She pushed to her feet as one of the MTs stepped over.

"Nothing we can do for her," he said. "She's cold. Must've been lying there for a couple hours before you found her. Fucking New York. People had to walk right by her."

"No." There were people now, crowding the sidewalk, ranged like a chorus for the dead. But there hadn't been . . . "No," Eve repeated. "We saw her fall."

"Body's cold," he repeated. "She's ninety if she's a day, and probably more than that. I don't see how she could've walked two feet with all those slices in her."

"I guess we'd better find out." She picked up her 'link, called it in.

CHAPTER
THREE

After cleaning the blood from her hands, she secured the scene, retrieved her field kit from the trunk. She was running the victim's prints when the first black and white rolled up.

"She's not in the database." Frustrated, Eve pushed to her feet, turned to the uniforms. "Keep these people back. Talk to them. Find out if anybody knew her, if anybody saw anything. There's a blood trail, and I don't want these people trampling all over it."

And where the hell were they, she wondered, when the woman was staggering down the street, bleeding to death? The street had been empty as the desert.

"What can I do?" Lopez asked her.

"Peabody's on her way — small slice of luck having a bunch of murder cops a few minutes away. I want you to give her a statement. Tell her everything you saw, everything you heard."

"She had an accent. Thick. Polish or Hungarian, maybe Romanian."

"Yeah, tell Peabody. Once you've done that, I can have one of the cops drive you where you need to go."

"If you need me to stay —"

"There's nothing more you can do here. I'll be in touch."

"I'd like to finish giving her Last Rites. I started, but . . . She's wearing a crucifix around her neck."

She debated. He'd already had his hands all over the body, and his clothes were stained, as hers were, with the old woman's blood. "Okay. You can do that while I start on her. Try to keep contact to a minimum."

"Your hand's bleeding a little."

"She dug in pretty hard with her nails. It's just a couple scratches."

Lopez knelt at the woman's head while Eve got gauges and tools out of her kit.

"Victim is Caucasian or possibly mixed race female of undetermined origin, age approximately ninety. Before expiring, she gave her name as Gizi. Multiple stab wounds," Eve continued, "chest, torso, arms. Looks like defensive wounds on the arms, the hands. She didn't just stand there and take it."

"She should have died at home, in her bed, surrounded by her children, grandchildren. I'm sorry," Lopez said when Eve glanced up. "I interrupted your record."

"Doesn't matter. And you're right."

"That's the difference between death and murder."

"It's the big one. Do her clothes look homemade to you?" As she asked, Eve turned up the hem on the long skirt with its wide stripes of color. "This looks handmade to me, and carefully done. She's wearing sandals — sturdy ones with some miles on them. Got a

158

tattoo, inside left ankle. Peacock feathers? I think they're peacock feathers."

"She's wearing a wedding ring. Sorry," Lopez said again.

"Yeah, wedding ring, or in any case a plain gold band, the cross pendant along with a second pendant, starburst pattern with a pale blue center stone, gold earrings. No bag, no purse, but if it were a violent mugging, why not take the jewelry?"

She slid her sealed hand into the pocket on the side of the skirt, closed her fingers over a little bag. It was snowy white, felt like silk, and tied precisely with silver cord in three knots.

She knew what it was even before she untied it and examined the contents. She'd seen this sort of thing before. "Woo-woo," she said to Lopez.

"What?"

"Magic stuff. Witchcraft or whatever. We got herbs, little crystals. I'd say she hedged her bets. Amulet and crucifix — and a spell deal in her pocket. Didn't help her."

Though she'd already noted time of death, she used her gauge to confirm. "Damn it, this thing must be broken. It's given me TOD at just past thirteen hundred. She died right here in front of us at sixteen-forty-two."

"Her skin's cold," Lopez murmured.

"We watched her die." Eve pushed to her feet, turning as Peabody jogged up, Morris in her wake.

"This wasn't on the party schedule," Peabody said as she looked at the body.

"I bet it wasn't on hers either." Eve took the weapon and harness she'd asked Peabody to bring, and after strapping it on covered it with the jacket her partner held out.

She sat on the curb, changed her skids for her boots.

"You need to get a statement from Father Lopez so we can spring him. Have one of the uniforms drive him back when you're done. You didn't have to come," she said to Morris. "I notified your people."

"I called them off. I'm right here, after all."

"Actually, I can use the head guy. My gauge is wonky. I recorded TOD as the damn TOD, since she died in front of me. But my gauge is putting it almost four hours earlier. Cause is pretty clear, but you might find something else. If you can take over on the body, I want to get on this blood trail, find the kill spot."

"Go ahead."

She followed the blood west.

The neighborhood was quiet. Maybe the heat kept people inside, she thought, or maybe most of them were at the sale at the Sky Mall or at the beach. But there was some pedestrian and street traffic.

Had no one seen a staggering, bleeding old woman and tried to help? Even for New York, that was too cold to believe. But the trail continued west for two blocks, right over crosswalks — as if the dying had felt obliged not to jaywalk. Then it headed north.

Buildings older here, she noted, squat towers of apartments and day flops, tiny markets and delis, the 24/7s, coffee shops, bakeries, and bodegas — and more people out and about on their Saturday business.

She continued another three blocks, then jogged north where the trail led into the mouth of a narrow alley between buildings.

And there, without question, was the kill spot.

Deep in the narrow trench, shadowed by overhangs, stinking of garbage from an overfilled recycler, blood splattered the pocked concrete walls, drenched the filthy ground.

She hitched open her field kit for a flashlight and played it over the walls, the ground, the neatly tied bag of trash beside the recycler.

"Did you tie that, Gizi? Bringing out the trash? Do you work here, live here? What were you doing in the alley otherwise? And how the hell did you walk better than six blocks after he sliced you to pieces? And why? Help would have been right around the corner."

Crouching, she unknotted the trash bag. Fruit and vegetable peelings, she noted, packaging from a small loaf of bread, an empty box of powdered milk, a long, slim bottle that had held some sort of wine . . .

She retied the bag, tagged it for evidence, and shifting it, found the key.

Old, heavy, she noted as she studied it. But then there were old buildings here that might still run to straight lock and key. She turned to the alley door and its keypad. Entrance digitally secured, but inside?

She'd have to see.

She bagged the key, labeled it, then walked back to the alley door and tried to see it.

Wants to take her trash out, comes out with her little bag, walked to the recycler.

Was he waiting for her? Why? Did she walk into an illegals deal?

Puts her bag down, turns — spatter says she'd turned, about three-quarters away from the wall when she was attacked. So he came from behind her, most likely. From the mouth of the alley or through the door behind her.

Eve positioned herself, started the turn from the wall. The first slice ripped the back of her right shoulder with a shock of pain that knocked her against the recycler. She grabbed for her weapon, swung to defend, but somehow the knife plunged into her back, once, twice. Dimly she heard something clink onto the ground, and thought: My key.

Then she was sliding down toward that filthy ground. But hands grabbed her, wrenched her around, shoved her hard against the wall. Through eyes glazed with shock and pain she saw the face of a demon — curling horns piercing the forehead, skin red as hellfire slashed with black and dirty gold. It bared its fierce teeth as the knife tore through her chest.

She put up her hands to fight, and the blade sliced them. She opened her mouth to scream, to curse, but had no voice.

As she fell, the only thought in her mind was Beata.

She came to coated with sweat. The hand holding her weapon shook as she slapped the other over her body looking for blood.

But she stood, unharmed, just as she'd been before she'd felt the first blow.

162

"What the hell was that?" Dizzy, she bent over, head between her knees until she got her breath back.

"Dallas? Hey!" Peabody rushed forward. "Are you okay?"

"Fine."

"Jeez, you're white as a ghost."

"I'm fine," she insisted. "It's the heat." To prove it, maybe to assure herself of it, she swiped the back of her hand over her sweaty brow. "Who's on scene?"

"Five uniforms, Morris. Crime scene got there before I left to follow you in." Peabody scanned the alley floor, the walls, the stinking recycler. "That's a hell of a lot of blood. How'd she manage to walk all that way after this?"

"Good question. It looks like she came down to take out her trash. The contents of the bag I tagged look like basic garbage from a single. And there was a key between it and the recycler. Could be hers, as it's about the only clean thing in here. Contact crime scene. We need them down here. Stick with the bag until they get here. I'm going to check the buildings. If that's her trash, she had to come from one of these two buildings."

She didn't draw a clean breath until she'd stepped out of the alley — and the instant she did, the shakes and dizziness vanished as if they'd never been.

She tried the ground-floor market first, moving past the displays of summer fruit and sleeves of flowers into the relative cool of the shop.

She walked to the counter where the woman sitting on a stool behind it greeted her with a wide smile. "Good afternoon. Can I help you find something?"

"NYPSD." Eve badged her. "Do you know a woman, in her nineties, gray hair — long, probably worn in a bun, dark eyes, olive complexion, five feet four, about a hundred and twenty pounds? Weathered face. Shows its miles. Heavy East European accent. Might wear a cross and an amulet with a blue stone."

"That sure sounds like Madam Szabo." The woman's smile faded. "Is she okay? She was just in this morning."

"Do you know where she lives?"

"In one of the weekly units above. On three, I think."

"Do you know her full name?"

"Ah, it's Gizi, Gizi Szabo. She's from Hungary. Is she in trouble?"

"She was attacked and killed this afternoon."

"Oh my God. Oh no. Wait." She pushed up, opened a door to what looked to be a tiny office/storeroom. "Zach. Zach, come out here. Somebody killed Madam Szabo."

"What are you talking about?" The man who stepped out wore an expression of annoyance along with a short-sleeved, collared shirt and knee shorts. "She's fine. We just saw her this morning."

"This is the police."

"Lieutenant Dallas, Homicide."

Annoyance dropped away into quick concern. "What the hell happened? Did somebody break into her place?"

"I'd like to check her unit, if you know the number. And I'll need your names."

"Karrie and Zach Morgenstern," the woman told her. "This is our place. Oh, Zach." Karrie curled a hand around his arm. "She stopped in here almost every day since she came."

"How long is that?"

"About a month maybe. She came to find her great-granddaughter. This is terrible; I can hardly take it in. I really liked her. She had such interesting stories — and she told my fortune once. She's — what is it, Zach?"

"Romany. A Gypsy. The real deal, too. She's in four D, Lieutenant. I carried some stuff up for her a couple times. Man, this is crap, you know that? Just crap. She was a sweetheart. Do you want me to take you up?"

"No, I'll find it. The alley between the buildings. This building uses that recycler?"

"Yeah. Damn thing's been broken for nearly a week, and we can't get them to come and . . ." Zach trailed off. "Is that where she was killed? In the alley? You mean we were right in here when . . ."

"Nothing you could've done. Is there anyone you know who gave her any trouble? Anyone who'd want to cause her harm?"

"I really don't." Zach looked at Karrie, got a shake of the head. "She was nice. Colorful. Did some fortune-telling out of her place."

"You said she was here to look for her great-granddaughter."

"Yes." Karrie sniffled, blinked at tears. "God, it's really hitting me. She came over — the granddaughter — about a year ago. She didn't live far from here, and

165

she came in a couple times. That's why Madam rented the place upstairs. Anyway, the granddaughter came to work, wanted to dance — on Broadway, like they all do, you know? Then about three months ago her family stopped hearing from her, couldn't reach her. And the place she worked waitressing said how she just stopped showing up. They contacted the police, but the cops didn't do much, I guess . . . Sorry."

"No need. Do you know the granddaughter's name?"

"Sure. Madam Szabo talked to everybody about her, put out flyers." Karrie continued as she reached under the counter, "She worked at Goulash — Hungarian restaurant a block west. We hand out flyers for her. You can have this. She's beautiful, isn't she? I think that's what her name means."

"Beata," Eve murmured, and felt as if her heart cracked in her chest. Such grief, such sorrow it almost took her to her knees as she studied the photo on the flyer.

The face that had been the light in the black.

"Ma'am? Um, Lieutenant? Are you okay?"

"Yeah. Thanks for your help. I may need to speak to you again."

"If we're not here, we live up on six. Six A, front of the building," Karrie told her. "Anything we can do."

"If you think of anything, you can contact me at Cop Central." Eve dug into her field kit for a card. "Anything strikes you."

Eve walked out just as Peabody approached. "Sweepers have the alley," she said.

"Vic was Gizi Szabo, and had a weekly unit on four. Claimed to be a Gypsy from Hungary."

"Wow. A real one?"

"Nobody claims to be a fake one," Eve returned, and felt herself steady a little. "Been here about three months, looking for a great-granddaughter who went missing." Eve used her master to access the apartment building's entrance. "Did some fortune-telling out of her place."

One glance at the ancient elevator had Eve choosing the stairs. She handed Peabody the flyer. "Run them both," she said. "Had Morris confirmed TOD before you left?"

"His TOD jibed with your gauge. Around one this afternoon."

"That's just bogus." And it infuriated her more than it should have. "I know when somebody dies when I've got my hands on their fricking heart, and I'm *talking* to them."

"Hungarian Gypsy fortune-teller. Maybe it's some sort of —"

"Don't even start with that voodoo, woo-woo, Free-Ager shit. She was alive, bleeding, and talking until about an hour ago."

At the door of 4 D, Eve took the key she'd found out of the evidence bag, slid it into the lock. And turned the knob.

CHAPTER
FOUR

It reminded her of her first apartment — the size, the age. That's what she told herself when struck, just for an instant, with a sharp sense of recognition.

The single room had no doubt been rented furnished, with a couple of cheap chairs and a daybed with a cracker-thin mattress, a chest — newly and brightly painted — that served as dresser and table.

Boldly patterned material had been fashioned into curtains for the single window, and with these and scarves and shawls draped over the faded chairs, spread over the narrow bed, the room took on a hopeful cheer.

One corner held a sink, AutoChef, friggie, all small-scale, along with a single cupboard. Another table stood there, painted a deep, glossy red under its fringed scarf. For seating, there were two backless stools.

Eve saw the old woman there, telling fortunes to those who sought to know their future.

"She made it nice," Peabody commented. "She didn't have a lot to work with, but she made it nice."

Eve opened the single, skinny closet, studied Szabo's neatly hung clothing, a single pair of sturdy walking shoes. Kneeling, she pulled two storage boxes out of the closet.

"Beata's things. Clothes, shoes, ballet gear, I'd say. A few pieces of jewelry, face and hair stuff. The landlord must have boxed it up when she didn't come back, didn't pay the rent."

It hurt, hurt to look through, to touch, to *feel* Beata as she dug through pretty blouses, skimmed over worn slippers.

She knew better, she reminded herself, knew better than to become personally involved. Beata Varga wasn't her victim, not directly.

The promise is in you.

The voice spoke insistently inside her head, inside her heart.

"Tag these," Eve ordered, shoving to her feet. She crossed over to the chest, studied the photo of Beata propped there and fronted by three scribed candles. Beside the photo a handful of colored crystals glittered in a small dish along with an ornate silver bell and a silver-backed hand mirror.

"What do we have on the granddaughter?" Eve asked.

"Beata Varga, age twenty-two. She's here on a work visa, and employed — until she went missing three months ago — at Goulash. No criminal. The family filed a report. A Detective Lloyd is listed as investigating officer. Missing Persons Division out of the One-three-six."

"Reach out there," Eve told her. "Have him meet us at the restaurant. Thirty minutes."

She opened the first drawer of the chest, found neatly folded underwear and nightclothes, and a box of carved wood. She lifted the lid, studied the pack of tarot cards, the peacock feather, the small crystal ball and stand.

Tools of her trade, Eve thought, started to set the box aside. Then, following impulse, pressed her thumbs over the carved flowers on the sides. Left, left, right. And a narrow drawer slid out of the base.

"Wow." Peabody leaned over her shoulder. "A secret drawer. Frosty. How did you open it?"

"Just . . . luck," Eve said, even as the hairs on the back of her neck stood up.

Inside lay a lock of dark hair tied with gold cord, a wand-shaped crystal on a chain, and a heart of white stone.

"They're hers." Eve's throat went dry and achy. "Beata's. Her hair, something she wore, something she touched."

"You're probably right. Szabo probably used them, along with the cards and crystals, maybe the bell and the mirror in locator spells. I'm not saying you can find people with spells," Peabody added when Eve just stared at her. "But that she thought she could. Anyway, Detective Lloyd's going to meet us."

"Then let's see what else we can find here first."

The old woman lived simply, neatly, and cautiously. In the cloth bag in the bottom of the chest Eve found a small amount of cash, another bag of crystals and herbs, a map of the city, and a subway card, along with ID and passport and a number of the flyers with Beata's image and information.

But taped under the friggie they found an envelope of cash with a peacock feather fixed diagonally across the seal.

"That's about ten thousand," Peabody estimated. "She didn't have to read palms to pay the rent."

"It's what she did. What kept her centered. Bag it, and let's seal this place up. We should get to the restaurant."

"She made it nice," Peabody repeated with another glance around. "I guess that's what travelers do. Make a home wherever they land, then pack it up and make the next one."

Beata hadn't packed it up, Eve thought, and wherever she was, it wasn't home.

Goulash did a bustling business on Saturday evening. Spices perfumed air that rang with voices and the clatter of silverware, the clink of glasses. The waitstaff wore red sashes at the waist of black uniforms while moving briskly from kitchen to table.

A rosy-cheeked woman of about forty offered Eve a welcoming smile. "Welcome to Goulash. Do you have a reservation?"

Eve palmed her badge. "We're not here for dinner."

"Beata! You've found her."

"No."

"Oh." The smile faded away. "I thought . . . I'm sorry, what can I do for you?"

"We're meeting Detective Lloyd on a police matter. We'll need somewhere to talk. And I'll need to speak with you and your staff."

"Of course." She looked around. "We're not going to have a table free for at least a half hour, but you can use the kitchen."

"That's fine. Your name?"

"Mirium Frido. This is my place, my husband's and mine. He's the chef. Is this about Beata? Beata Varga?"

"Indirectly."

"Give me one minute to put someone else on the door." Mirium hurried over to one of the waitresses. The girl glanced at Eve and Peabody, nodded.

Mirium signaled Eve forward, then led them through the dining room, past the bar, and through one of a pair of swinging doors into the chaos of the kitchen.

"Dinner rush. I'll set you up over here — our chef's table. Jan invites customers back sometimes — gives them a treat. I told Vee to send Detective Lloyd back when he gets here. He's been in several times about Beata, so everyone knows him. Can you tell me anything about her? Do you have more information?"

"I'll know more when I speak with the detective. She worked for you."

"Yes. A beautiful girl and a good worker. She was a pleasure." Mirium reached back to a shelf, picked up three setups, and arranged them on the table. "I know they think she just took off — Gypsy feet — but it doesn't make sense. She made amazing tips — the looks, the voice, the personality. And . . . well, she just wouldn't be that rude and careless, wouldn't have left without telling us. Or her family."

"Boyfriend?"

"No. Nothing serious and no one specific. She dated — she's young and gorgeous. But she was serious about her dancing. Went to auditions, took classes every day. She had an understudy spot in a small musical review. And she'd just landed a part in the chorus on a new musical spot off-Broadway. There wasn't enough time for a serious boyfriend. I'm sorry, please sit. How about some food?"

"We're good, thanks. You have flyers at the reservation station, I noticed."

"Yes. Her grandmother — well, great-grandmother — is here from Hungary. She had them made up and takes them around the city. She comes by here every day. Detective —"

"Lieutenant," Eve said automatically.

"Lieutenant, Beata worked here nearly a year. You get to know people who work for you, and I promise you, she wouldn't worry her family this way. I'm so afraid something's happened to her. I know Madam Szabo's determined to find her, but with every day that passes . . ."

"I'm sorry to tell you Gizi Szabo was killed this afternoon."

"No." Instantly Mirium's eyes filled. "Oh, no. What happened?"

"We're going to find out."

"She told my fortune," Mirium murmured. "Said I would have a child, a son. Jan and I haven't . . . That was two months ago. I found out yesterday I'm pregnant. I told her just today."

"She was in today."

173

"Yes, about eleven, I guess." Shaking her head, Mirium swiped at a tear while the kitchen bustle raged on around them. "She was so happy for me. She said she'd felt his search, my son's. An old soul, she said, who'd turned the wheel again. She talked like that," Mirium murmured. "I don't really believe that sort of thing, but when she looks at you . . . She's — she was — Romany, and a speaker for the dead."

So am I, Eve thought with a quick chill. I speak for the dead. "What time did she leave?"

"She was only here a few minutes. She said she was going home. She said she felt closer to Beata, felt something coming. Or someone. I don't know, she was — I want to say optimistic. She was going to rest and then do a new spell because she was breaking through, well, the veil. She said Beata was toward the setting sun, below the rays, um, locked beyond the red door. I have no idea what that meant," Mirium added. "Or if it meant anything, but she was *fierce* about it. She swore Beata was alive, but trapped. By a devil.

"I know how that sounds," she continued. "But —" She glanced over. "Here's Detective Lloyd. Sorry I went on like that."

"Don't be," Eve told her. "Every detail, every impression, is helpful."

"I just can't believe Madam's gone. She was such a presence, even for the short time I knew her. Excuse me. I need to tell Jan. Hello, Detective Lloyd, have a seat."

Lloyd was a square-faced, square-bodied man who transmitted *I'm* a *cop* from thirty paces. He gave Eve and Peabody a brisk nod, then sat at the little square table. Shook hands.

"It's too bad about the old lady. She had some juice, had some spine. She should've stayed back home."

She made home where she landed, Eve thought, remembering Peabody's take. "Tell me about Beata Varga."

He hitched up a hip, took a disc out of his pocket. "I went ahead and made a copy of the file for you."

"Appreciate it."

"She's a looker. Smart, from what I get, savvy, but still green when it comes to city. Used to wandering with her family — tribe, you'd say. Came here wanting to be a Broadway star, and the family wasn't happy about it."

"Is that so?"

"Wanted her home. Wanted her to stay pure, you could say. Get hitched, have babies, keep the line going, that sort of thing. But, the old woman — Szabo — overruled them. She wanted the girl to take her shot, find her destiny, like that. The girl got a job here and a place a couple blocks away. Started taking classes — dance classes, acting classes, stuff like that, at West Side School for the Arts. Went to the cattle calls regular. No boyfriend — or not one in particular. Dated a few guys. I got the names and statements, the data in the file there." He nodded toward the disc. "Nobody rang the bell."

He paused when Mirium came over with a tray holding three tall glasses. "I don't mean to interrupt.

Just something cold to drink while you talk. If you need me for anything, I'll be out front."

"They're good people," Lloyd commented when she left them. "Her, her husband. They come up clean. Ran the whole staff when I caught the case. Got some bumps here and there, but nobody popped."

"What's the time line?"

When he didn't refer to his notes, Eve knew the case had him, and his teeth were still in it.

"Beata Varga went to her regular dance class, eight a.m. to ten. Hit a rehearsal for the show she just landed at Carmine Theater on Tenth at eleven. Reported here for work at one, all excited about the show. Worked a split shift, so she was off at three, hit her acting class from three thirty to five, back to work at five thirty, off at eleven. Walked down the block with a couple friends from work — names in the file — then split off to go home. That's the last anyone can verify seeing her. Eleven ten, then poof.

"Apartment's not big on security. No cams," he added. "No log-in. The neighbors can't say whether she came in that night, but nobody saw her. A bag and some of her clothes and personal items are gone, and there was no money in the place. According to statements, she pulled in hefty tips and was saving. It looks like she got itchy feet, tossed what she wanted in a bag, and took off."

"That's not what you think," Eve said, watching his eyes.

"Nope. I think between here and home she ran into trouble. Somebody snatched her. I think she's been dead since that night. You know as well as I do, Lieutenant, we don't always find the bodies."

No, Eve thought. "If she's dead, then someone she knew killed her. Why else try to make it seem like she took off? Why pack clothes?"

"I lean that way, but I can't find anything." Frustration rippled around him. "It could be whoever did her used her ID for her address, had her key — she carried all that in her purse. Tried to cover it up. I'm still working it, when I can, as an MP, but my sense is it's more in your line."

He glanced around as he sipped his drink. "The old woman didn't buy it for cheap," he said. "Claimed she talked to the dead, and if the girl was dead, she'd know. I don't buy that for free, but . . . Now the old woman gets murdered? People get dead in the city," he added as he set his glass down. "But it's got a smell to it. I'd appreciate you giving me what you've got on it. Something or somebody might cross somewhere."

"You'll get it," Eve promised. Because something or somebody *would* cross.

CHAPTER
FIVE

The ballet studio ranged over the fourth floor of an old building on the West Side. Under the glare of street lights the pocked bricks were dull and grayed with time and pollution, but the glass in every window sparkled.

Out of Order signs hung on the chipped gray doors of both elevators. Students, staff, and visitors had expressed their opinions on the situation with varying degrees of humor or annoyance by tagging the doors with obscenities, anatomically impossible suggestions, and illustrations on how to attempt the suggestions. All in a variety of languages.

"Guess they've been out of order for a while," Peabody commented.

Eve just stared at one of the series of strange symbols and letters while her mind — something in there — translated it with a kind of dry humor.

"Fuck your mother," she murmured, and Peabody blinked.

"What? Why?"

"Not *your* mother."

"But you just said —"

Eve shook her head impatiently. "It's Russian. A classic Russian insult." She reached out, ran a fingertip over the lettering on the door. "*Yob tvoiu mat.*"

Peabody studied the phrase Eve traced and thought it might as well be hieroglyphics. "How do you know that?"

"I must have seen it somewhere else." But that didn't explain how she knew — knew — the elevators had been down for weeks. Turning away, she started up the stairs.

Nor could she say why her heart began to beat faster as they climbed, passed the other studios and classrooms. Tap, jazz, children's ballet sessions. Or why, as she approached the fourth floor, the music drifting out hit some chord inside her.

She followed the music, stepped into the doorway.

The woman was whiplash thin in her black leotard and gauzy skirt. Her hair, wildly red, slicked back from a face that struck Eve as thirty years older than her body. Her skin was white as the moon, her lips red as her hair.

She called out in French to a group of dancers at a long bar who responded by sliding their feet from one position to another — pointed toes, flat feet, lifted leg, bended knees.

In a corner of the studio a man played a bright and steady beat on an old piano. He seemed to look at nothing at all with a half smile on his face, dark eyes dreamy in a sharp-featured face surrounded by dark hair with wide, dramatic white streaks.

As Eve and Peabody entered the room, one of the dancers, a man in his twenties, dark hair restrained in a curling tail, turned his head a fraction to stare, to scowl.

Interesting, she thought, a guy wearing a leotard and ballet shoes would make a couple of cops so quickly.

The woman stopped, planted her hands on her hips. "You want lessons, you sign up. Class has started."

Eve merely held up her badge.

The woman sighed hugely. "Alexi, take the class."

At the order, the scowling man tossed his head, sniffed, then strode out from the bar. The woman gestured them into the hallway.

"What could you want?" she demanded in a voice husky, impatient, and thick with her homeland. "I'm teaching."

"Natalya Barinova?"

"Yes, yes. I am Barinova. What do I want with police?"

"You know a Gizi Szabo?"

"Yes, yes," she said in the same dismissive tone. "She looks for Beata, who ran off to Las Vegas."

"You know Beata Varga went to Vegas?" Eve demanded.

"Where else? They think, these girls, they go make big money showing their tits and wearing big feathers on their heads. They don't want to work, to sweat, to suffer, to *learn*."

"Beata told you she was leaving?"

"No, she tells me nothing, that girl. But she doesn't come back. She's not the first, will not be the last. Her old grandmother comes — a good woman — looking for this flighty girl who has talent. Wasted now. Wasted."

The way she cut her hand through the air made her anger clear.

"I tell her this, tell Gizi, Beata has talent. Needs discipline, needs practice. Should not waste so much time with the tap and the jazz and the *modern* business. I tell Beata the same, but she only smiles. Then poof, off she runs."

"When did you last see Madam Szabo?"

"Ah . . ." Barinova frowned, waved a hand in the air. "A day ago, I think. Yes, on yesterday. She comes often. Sometimes we have tea. She was a dancer in her day, she tells me, and we talk. She's a good woman, and Beata shows no respect to her. She thinks harm has come to Beata, but I say how could this be? Beata is strong and smart — except she's stupid to run to Las Vegas. So, she asked you to come? Like the other police?"

"No. Madam Szabo was killed this afternoon."

"No." Barinova held out both hands as if to push the words away. "No. How does this happen?"

"She was stabbed in the alley outside her apartment building."

Barinova closed her eyes. "Such cruelty. I will pray she finds peace and her killer roasts in hell. Beata must bear some blame for this. Selfish girl."

"When did you last see Beata?"

"Ah." She cut a hand through the air again, but now there were tears in her eyes for the old woman and disgust for the young. "Weeks now, maybe months. She

181

comes to class excited about a part in some musical. She works hard, this is true. I give her the pas de deux with Alexi in our autumn gala. My son," she added. "She dances well with him in practice, then she says she has this part — maybe she does, maybe she doesn't. But soon after, she doesn't come to class anymore. I have my brother Sasha to call her on the 'link, but she doesn't answer. We tell all this to the police when they come."

"Did Madam Szabo tell you she was concerned about anyone? That she had any leads on Beata?"

"She said the last she was here she believed Beata was close. She was Romany, you understand, and had a gift. Me, I have Romany in my blood, but from long ago. She used her gift and said Beata was close, but trapped. Below, behind a red door." Barinova shrugged. "She was very old, and gifted, yes, but sometimes hope and wishes outweigh truth. The girl ran off as girls do, and now a good woman is dead."

"It would be helpful if we could talk to your son and brother, maybe some of the students who took classes with Beata."

"Yes, yes, we will help. I will miss tea with Gizi and our talks." She turned back into the studio, moved to her son. She spoke quickly in Russian, gestured, then took his place as he strode out.

"You're interrupting my practice." Unlike his mother, he had no trace of an accent. What he had was attitude.

"Yeah, murder interrupts a lot of things."

182

"What murder?" His sneer twisted off his face. "Beata? She's dead?"

"I don't know, but her great-grandmother is."

"Madam Szabo?" His shock looked sincere enough, and so, Eve noted, did his relief. "Why would anybody kill an old woman?"

"People always seem to have a reason. In this case, maybe because she was getting close to finding out what happened to Beata."

"Beata left." He jerked a shoulder sharply. "She didn't have what it takes."

"To what?"

"To dance, to live life full."

Eve cocked her head. "Wouldn't sleep with you?"

He tipped back his head to look down his long nose. "I don't have a problem getting women into bed. If we'd danced together for the gala, we'd sleep together. One is like the other."

"I thought you did dance together."

"Practice."

"So it must've annoyed you that she wouldn't have sex with you."

"This woman, that woman." He smiled slowly. "One is like the other."

"Charming. When did you last see Madam Szabo?"

"Just yesterday. She'd visit class, and my mother, a lot. Talk to the other dancers here, and the other studios down on two and three where Beata took some classes. She'd have tea with my mother, sit with my uncle at the piano. She said she felt close to Beata here."

183

"And she mentioned something about Beata being close. Being below."

"She was a Gypsy — and took it seriously. I don't buy into that, but yeah, she said some stuff about it. Didn't make any sense, because if Beata was close, why did she stop coming to class? Why did she bail on the part she got, and screw the understudy position she had? Dancers dance. She took off, that's what she did, to dance somewhere else. Found a bigger brass ring to grab."

"Where were you today, Alexi? Say from noon to four?"

"Cops." He sniffed again. "I slept late in the apartment of Allie Madison. She and I will dance in the gala, and she and I sleep together. For now," he added. "We stayed in bed until about two, then met friends for a little brunch. Then we came here, to practice, then to take class. She's the blonde, the tall one with the tattoo of a lark on her left shoulder blade. I need to practice."

"Go ahead. Ask your uncle to come out."

Eve waited until he'd strode off again. "Did you run him?" she asked Peabody.

"Oh yeah. He's got a few drunk and disorderlies, a couple of minor illegals possessions, an assault — bar fight, which added destruction of private property, public nuisance, resisting. He's twenty-six, listed as principal dancer and instructor here at the school, and lives with his mother upstairs on six."

Got a temper, Eve thought as the piano player stepped out.

"Officer?"

"Lieutenant Dallas, Detective Peabody. And you're Sasha?"

"Sasha Korchov, yes. My nephew said you came because Madam Szabo was killed." His dreamy eyes were soft and sad, like this voice. Like the slow glide of a bow over violin strings. "I'm very sorry to know this."

"Were you here when she came in yesterday?"

"I didn't see her. Natalya was using the music disc — advanced students to work on dances for the gala. I am in the storeroom, I think, with the props when she was here. My sister tells me I missed her. We enjoyed talking music and dance. I saw her the day before, on the street, not far from here. I was going to the market. But she was across the street and didn't hear when I called out to her. We talked in Russian," he said with a ghost of a smile. "Her mother was Russian, like mine and my papa, so sometimes we talked in Russian. I will miss it, and her."

"What about Beata?"

"Beata." He sighed. "My sister, she thinks Beata ran off to Las Vegas, but no, I think something bad happened to her. I don't say so to Gizi, but . . . I think she knows I believe this. She could see inside if she looked, so I think sometimes she was sad to talk to me. I'm sorry for it."

"What did you think happened to Beata?"

"I think she loved her family, and to dance, and New York. I don't think she would leave all of that by choice. I think she's dead, and now so is Gizi. Now Gizi will find her, so they will, at least, have each other."

"Your nephew was interested in Beata — personally."

"He likes pretty girls," Sasha said cautiously. "What young man doesn't?"

"But she wasn't interested in him?"

"She was more interested in dance than in men. Pure of heart, and with music in her blood."

"Can you tell me where you were this afternoon?"

"I went to market after morning classes — I like to go most days. I came home to have my lunch and to play. I opened the windows so the music could go out. I came down to talk to my sister, and play for the two o'clock class. When that's done, we have tea, Natalya and me."

"Okay, thank you. Would you send Allie Madison out?"

"Will they send her body home?"

"I don't have that information."

"I hope she goes home," Sasha murmured, then wandered back inside.

"He immigrated here from Russia with his sister and her kid — Alexi was a couple months old — twenty-six years ago," Peabody added. "Sister's husband's listed as dead, right before the kid was born. Korchov was thirty-five and had been a big-deal ballet guy until he got messed up in a car wreck. They fixed him, but his career was shot. The sister was thirty, and had a pretty decent career herself. They opened the school. He has his own apartment on six. No criminal record. No marriages on record, two cohabs, both in Russia. The second one died in the same wreck that messed him up."

"Okay." Eve watched the willowy blonde glide out.

"You wanted to see me?" She had a breathy, baby doll voice that made Eve think it was Allie's good luck ballet didn't require vocals.

"Just verifying some information. Would you mind telling me where you were this afternoon?"

"Sure. Alex and I had brunch with some friends at Quazar's. Caviar and champagne — it was CeeCee's birthday — which probably wasn't a good idea right before practice. I'm still carrying those blinis." She smiled easily. "Doesn't bother Alex, I guess, because he jumped right in when we got here. Pushed me through that damn pas de deux until I thought about just sticking my fingers down my throat. But Barinova will skin you for purging, and she always knows. Anyway, I got through it. My Angel to his Devil."

"His what?"

"Devil." She lifted the water bottle she carried, took a long sip. "We're performing the final pas de deux from *Diabolique*. I'm dancing Angel. Alex is Devil. Let me tell you, it's a killer."

Eve looked past her to the studio doorway. "I just bet."

CHAPTER
SIX

"That's what I'd call a devil of a coincidence," Peabody commented when they stepped out on the street.

"Are you buying it?"

"Not even for the couple of loose credits in my pocket."

"I want you to check with the other people the blonde gave us, and the restaurant. We'll see if Alexi could've managed to slip away. See what the timing is from the restaurant to the alley, from the school to the alley."

"Beata turned him down, pissed him off. He kills her, buries the body." Peabody scanned the area. "God knows where, but that would fit in with the west of the alley, underground deal."

"She's not dead. She's trapped." Eve snapped it out furiously, shocking herself as much as Peabody.

"Okay . . . So you think —"

"It's what she thought. Szabo." Eve rubbed a hand between her breasts where her heart beat, hard and dull, a hammer against cloth. "I'm saying Szabo thought Beata was alive."

"Right. Behind a red door. Why do people have to be so cryptic?"

188

Think like a cop, Eve ordered herself. Facts, logic, instinct. "Szabo spends time at the school, with Alexi et al, sniffs it out, suspects, hints around. Maybe trying to get Alexi to make a move. He kills her." Eve rolled it around. "Awful damn tidy, but sometimes it just is."

"Well, the old lady told everybody Beata was still alive, so that doesn't ride the train very well."

"She poofs. She's got a job, her classes, landed a part. Sounds like everything's working out for her, but she poofs. Odds are she didn't poof voluntarily — that's Lloyd's take, and I agree."

"Three months is a long time," Peabody put in. "A long time to hold somebody who doesn't want to be held. And for what reason?"

"Szabo didn't want to believe the girl was dead, and who can blame her?" Eve added. "Not only her great-granddaughter, but she overrode the rest of the family so Beata could come to New York."

"Had to feel sick about it." Like Eve, Peabody scanned the street, the buildings, the traffic. "What did she say exactly? To you, I mean."

Eve didn't want to go back there, to kneeling in the street, the woman's hand clasped with hers. Blood to blood.

"She said Beata's name, she said she was trapped, couldn't get out. The below bit, the red door. She asked for help."

You are the warrior. I am the promise.

Fighting to stay steady, Eve shoved a hand through her hair. "She was dying."

But her eyes, Eve remembered, had been alert, alive.

"We comb through the alibis, check her other habitats." Do the work, Eve thought, take the steps. "I'm going to check in with Morris, contact the arresting officers about Alexi, get their take on him."

"Beata's disappearance and the old woman's murder — if they're not connected, it's another devil of a coincidence."

"We pursue the investigation as if they are. We figure out one, we've got the other."

"I could tag McNab, have him meet me, go by the theater where she was supposed to work. Lloyd covered it," Peabody added, "but we could try fresh eyes on it."

"Good thinking. Send me whatever you get."

She needed thinking time, Eve told herself as they split up. A stop at the morgue to confirm TOD — which was just stupid, since she'd been right there at TOD — to see if Morris or the lab had been able to get a handle on the type of blade used, if the sweepers had found any trace evidence.

Deal with the facts first, she thought as she got in her vehicle — then move on to theory. But she sat a moment, suddenly tired, suddenly angry. It felt as if something pushed inside her brain, trying to shove her thoughts into tangents.

Not enough downtime, she decided. No time to take some good, deep breaths between cases. So she took them now, just closing her eyes for a moment, ordering her mind and body to clear.

Alive. Trapped. Help.

Keep your promise!

The voice was so clear in her head she jerked up, had a hand on her weapon as she swiveled to check the seat beside her, behind her. Her heart pounded painfully against her ribs, in her throat, in her ears as she lowered her unsteady hand.

"Stop. Just stop," she ordered herself. "Do what you have to do, then get some sleep." She pulled away from the curb, but gave in to need and called home.

And her heart slowed, settled a little when Roarke's face flowed on-screen.

"Lieutenant, I was hoping I'd — What's wrong?"

"Nothing. Well, nothing except having some old Hungarian woman bleed out under my hands. Tired," she admitted. "I've got to head down to the morgue because there was a glitch with the TOD. I need to get it straightened out, then talk to a bunch of cops about a Russian ballet guy. Sorry," she added. "This one literally fell in my lap."

"I'll meet you at the morgue."

"Why?"

"Where else does a man meet his wife — when they're you and me?" She looked pale, he thought, her eyes too dark against her skin.

"Yeah, okay. I'll see you there."

When she broke transmission, Roarke stared at the blank screen of his 'link. Not even a token protest? More than tired, he thought.

His lieutenant was not herself.

She got lost. She would have deemed it impossible, but she couldn't find her way. The streets seemed too crowded, too confusing, and the blare of horns when she hesitated at a light had her jumping in her seat. Frustration turned to sweaty fear that ran a snaking line down the center of her back. Battling it back, she ordered the dash navigator to plot her route, then gave in and put her vehicle on auto.

Tired, she assured herself and closed her eyes. Just tired. But there was a lingering unease that she was ill — or worse.

Need a boost, she thought, nearly shuddering with relief as she arrived at the morgue. She'd grab a tube of Pepsi at Vending, down some caffeine. Maybe even choke down a PowerBar because, Jesus, she was starving.

What was wrong with the air in here? she wondered as she started down the white tunnel. The lights glaring off the tiles slapped into her eyes and made them ache. It was frigid, an icy blast after the heat of the summer night. Yet under her chilled skin her blood beat hot, like a fever raging.

She headed for Vending, digging into her pockets, her mind on food and caffeine. A woman sat on the floor beside the machines, her face in her hands, weeping.

"I'm scared. I'm scared," she repeated. "Nobody sees me now."

"What's the problem?" As Eve crouched down, the woman dropped her hands. Her face, livid with bruising, shone with shock and what might have been hope.

"You can see me?"

"Of course I can see you. You need medical attention. Take it easy. I'm going to get someone, then —"

"It's too late." Tears ran down the swollen face as the woman dipped her head again. "Look what he did to me."

Eve froze as she stared at the gaping wound on the back of the woman's head, at the dried blood matting the hair, soaking the blouse.

"Hold on. Just —" Eve reached out, and her hand passed through the woman's arm. "Jesus God."

"It was Rennie." Sniffling, she pushed the heels of her hands through the tears.

"What are you? What is this?"

"I don't know, but I have to tell *somebody*. It was Rennie," she repeated. "The bastard. He was mad at me 'cause I helped Sara get away from him. He must've followed me from work, and when I was in the park, he was just there. And he yelled and he hit me. He kept hitting me, and I couldn't get away. Nobody came to help. Nobody saw, and he hit me and hit me, and I fell. And he picked up a rock and he killed me. It's not right. What am I going to do now? I'm scared to be here. I'm scared to be dead."

Eve couldn't swallow, could barely breathe. "This has to stop."

"Rennie killed me."

The woman — the hallucination — held out her hands. Tore them up, Eve thought in some cold part of her brain. Tore them up when she fell, when she tried to crawl away.

"He killed me, and now I won't ever get married or eat ice cream or buy new shoes and have drinks with Sara. Rennie Foster killed me with a rock in Riverside Park, and maybe he'll kill Sara next. What's going to happen?"

"I don't know."

"Aren't I supposed to go somewhere? I don't want to stay here. It's cold here. It's too cold and it's too bright. Can you help me? I'm Janna, Janna Dorchester, and I didn't do anything wrong. Is this hell?"

"No." But she wasn't entirely sure.

Maybe hell was cold and bright. Maybe hell was losing your mind.

"Eve." Roarke dropped down beside her, took her arms. "Christ, you're burning up. Come on now."

He started to lift her, but she resisted. "No. Wait." She sucked in a breath, shuddered it out. "You don't see her?"

He pressed a hand to her forehead. "I see you, sitting on the floor of the morgue looking like a ghost."

"At one," she murmured.

"I guess he can't see me because I'm dead and everything," Janna said. "Why do you?"

"I don't know. I need Morris," she told Roarke. "And God, I need something to drink."

"Don't leave me," Janna begged, dropping her head again so Eve could see the ugly wound that killed her. "Please don't leave me here alone."

"I'm just going to sit here. Bring Morris, will you? I just . . . need to sit here." Deal, she ordered herself.

Deal with what's in front of you, then figure out the rest. "Could really use something cold to drink."

Roarke rose, cursing under his breath as he ordered a tube of Pepsi.

"He's gorgeous." Janna smiled a little even as she knuckled at tears. "Mega frosted. Is he your boyfriend?"

"We're married," Eve murmured.

"Seriously icy for you," Janna said as Roarke glanced down.

"So we are," he said. "And I'll be taking my wife to a doctor in short order. I'll get you Morris first, but then you're done here."

"He's got a really sexy voice, too." Janna sighed as Eve took the tube Roarke had opened, drank.

"Thanks. I'm going to sit right here," she said as much to Janna as Roarke, "while you get Morris."

And while she sat wondering if she had a brain tumor or had dropped into some strange, vivid dream, she put on the cop and interviewed the dead.

Minutes later, Morris hurried down the tunnel with Roarke.

"Dallas." He knelt, laid a hand on her brow as Roarke had. "You're feverish."

"Just tell me if you've gotten a body in — female, mixed race, midtwenties, ID'd as Janna Dorchester. Beating death in Riverside Park."

"Yes. She's only just come in. How did you —"

"Who caught the case?"

"Ah . . . Stuben's primary."

"I need to contact him. Can you get me his contact data?"

"Of course. But you don't look well."

"I'm feeling better, actually." Odd, she thought, how the cop approach steadied her, even when her interviewee was dead. "I think I'll feel better yet once I talk to Stuben. I'd appreciate it, Morris."

"Give me a minute."

"Eve." Roarke took her hand as Morris strode away. "What's going on here?"

"I'm not sure, and I need you to give me a really open mind. I mean wide-open. Yours is already more open than mine about, you know, weird stuff."

"What sort of weird stuff is my mind going to be wide-open about?"

"Okay." She looked into his eyes, so blue, so beautiful. Eyes she trusted with everything she had. "There's a dead woman sitting right beside me. Her name's Janna Dorchester, and some asshole named Rennie Foster bashed her head in with a rock in Riverside Park. She's worried her friend Sara might be next on his list. So I'm going to pass the information to the primary. I can read Russian."

"I'm sorry?"

"I can read Russian. I think I can speak it, too, and I'm pretty sure I can make Hungarian goulash. And maybe borscht, possibly pierogies. The old woman, the one who fell into my lap and happened to be a Gypsy speaker for the dead, did something to me. Or I have a brain tumor."

Staring into her eyes, Roarke cupped Eve's face in his hands. "*Kak vashi dela?*"

"*U menya vsyo po pnezhne mu.* Hey, you speak Russian?"

He sat back on his heels, rocked right down to the bone. "A handful of phrases, and certainly not as fluently as you, apparently. And despite your answer, I doubt you're fine."

They looked up as Morris came back. "I have what you need."

"Great." Eve took out her 'link, and staying where she was, contacted Detective Stuben. "Lieutenant Dallas," she said, "Homicide, out of Central. I've got some information on your vic, on Janna Dorchester." She looked at Janna as she spoke. "You're going to want to find Rennie Foster and get some protection to a Sara Jasper. Let me lay it out for you."

When she had, she answered his question on how she came by the information by claiming a confidential informant.

"Unless Stuben's an idiot — and he didn't strike me that way — that should do it." Eve got to her feet. "It's all I can do."

"I'm still dead, but I'm not as scared. It's not so cold anymore."

"I don't think you have to stay here."

"Maybe for a little while. It helped to talk to you. I still wish I wasn't dead, but . . ." She trailed off, shrugged.

"Good luck." Eve turned to Morris. "I don't know how to explain it. I need to see Gizi Szabo."

"Dallas, did you just have a conversation with the dead?"

"It sure felt that way. And I'd really appreciate it if you wouldn't spread it around. I need to work, I need to keep going, or I'm pretty sure I'm going to go crazy. So . . ." She started forward, glanced back, and saw Janna lift a hand in good-bye. "I need to confirm TOD on Szabo."

"I've run it three times, using various components. It's still thirteen hundred."

"It's not possible." She shoved through the doors of the autopsy suite. "I was *there*. Lopez was there, hours later. She fell off the curb, we administered first aid. She —"

"Eve," Roarke interrupted, "you just spoke with a woman killed more than two hours ago, and you're questioning the possible?"

"I know the difference between dead and alive." She stepped up to the body. "Why can't I see *her*? Why can't I talk to *her*? I look at her, and I feel . . . rage and frustration. And . . . obligation."

"I spoke with Chale," Morris told her. At the sink he ran cold water over a cloth, wrung it out. Then he came to her and smoothed it over her face himself to cool it.

"He said the same, but he also said that she took your hand, spoke to you, and there was a light — a blast of light and energy. And for a moment after it, you seemed to be blank. Just blank. He said something seemed to pass between you."

She took the cloth, mildly embarrassed he'd tended to her — that she'd let him. "You don't believe that kind of thing."

198

"The science says this woman died at one this afternoon — irrefutably — but there's more in the world than science."

Maybe, she thought — hard to argue about it right at the moment. But it had been routine and order that had gotten her through the experience with Janna. So she'd stay there as long as she could.

"Let's stick with science for the moment. What can you tell me about the weapon?"

"All right. A thin, double-edged blade. Seven and a quarter inches in length." He turned to a screen to bring up the image he'd reconstructed from the wounds, then turned back to the body. "You see here where the killer thrust it fully into her, the bruising from the bolster."

She leaned in, studying the gouges, the slices. "A dagger."

"Yes. He hit bone. The tip will be chipped." Morris showed her a tiny piece of steel, sealed in a tray. "I recovered this."

"Okay, that's good. He stabbed her in the back first — back of the shoulder." She remembered the shocking, tearing pain. "Because he's a coward, and because he feared her. She didn't see his face — he wore a mask or makeup. A kind of costume, because he's theatrical. A devil," she murmured, "because it's a role he plays, or wants to. Because it's powerful, because it instills fear, because he wanted that image to be the last she saw."

"Why?" Morris asked.

"He has something she wanted, and she wouldn't have stopped until she got it back. Exposed him. Punished him. Deprived him."

"Now you'll get it back."

She turned to Roarke, nodded. "Yeah. I will. I need to go home. You could drive while I talk to some cops."

"Dallas," Morris said, "I'd like to talk about this at some point."

"Yeah. At some point." She hesitated, handed him back the cloth, then closed her hand over his for just a moment. "Thanks."

Cooler, steadier, she walked down the tunnel with Roarke.

"Is she there?"

Eve paused, looked down at the floor where she'd sat with Jenna. "No. I guess she's gone wherever she had to go. Jesus, Roarke."

He took her hand firmly. "Let's get to the bottom of this, because right now I don't know if you need a doctor or a bloody priest."

"A priest?"

"For an exorcism."

"That's not funny," she muttered.

"It's not, no."

CHAPTER
SEVEN

Roarke gave her the time she needed while he drove. He said nothing, listening to her talk with a handful of cops about someone named Alexi Barin. Since her color was back, and her skin no longer felt as though it might burn off her bones, he checked the impulse to take her straight to a health center.

He considered his wife, among other things, cynical, stable, and often annoyingly rooted in reality and logic.

When she told him, straight-faced and clear-eyed, she'd had a conversation with the dead, he leaned toward believing her. Particularly adding in her unhesitating response to his simple *How are you?* in Russian.

She clicked off her 'link again, said, "Hmmm."

"How do you make Hungarian goulash?"

"What? I'm not making goulash."

"I didn't ask you to make it, but how you would."

"Oh, it's a test. Well, you'd cut up some onions and brown them in hot oil — just to golden brown, then you'd take this beef you'd cut in cubes and coated with flour, add that and some paprika to the oil and onions. Then —"

"That's enough."

"Why would you coat good meat with flour? I thought flour was for baking stuff."

"Which proves you know less about cooking than I do, which is next to nothing, and yet you can toss off a recipe for goulash."

"It's weird, and it's pretty fucking irritating. Which is why I'm going home instead of in to Central. I'm not going to find myself talking to some dead guy or whatever in front of other cops."

"You're still you," he murmured, foolishly relieved. "You're more embarrassed than frightened by the situation you appear to be in."

"I don't even believe this is happening, but I know it is. I'm not sure I wouldn't rather have a brain tumor."

She took a breath, then another. "I'm going back over it in my head. She was walking — staggering — bleeding all over the place. Science says she was dead, but Lopez saw her, too — and the medics when they got there. She talked to me. She looked at me."

She moved back to the scene. "But she'd walked that way for blocks — I followed the blood trail back. And no one helped her, no one called for help. I can't buy that, so, using the twisted logic of this whole deal, I have to conclude no one saw her."

"Continuing with that so-called twisted logic, she came to you. She had enough left in her to cross your path, to leave you a trail, to give you what you'd need to help her."

"You could theorize. And the first thing she said was the girl's name: Beata. That she was trapped, needed

202

help. She told me her name, and when I asked who'd done this to her, she said the devil. And . . ."

"What?"

"She said I was the warrior. Her eyes were so dark, black eyes, so intense. She said I had to take her in, let her in. She asked me, begged me. Take me in, so I said sure. I just wanted to keep her calm and alive until the MTs got there."

"You agreed."

"I guess I did." Huffing out a breath, she dragged a hand through her hair. "I guess I did, then she grabbed my hand, and bam — blinding light and like this electrical shock. These voices. I saw her face — the girl — Beata. Next thing I know, Lopez is calling my name, the medics are there, and Szabo's dead. Cold and dead."

"Because, scientifically at least, she'd died hours earlier."

"It's fucked up," was Eve's opinion. "I felt shaky and off. I guess I haven't felt all the way steady since. I recognized things I shouldn't have and didn't recognize things I should. God, Roarke, I got lost driving to the morgue. I just couldn't remember the streets."

He thought of how she'd looked, face dead white, shiny with sweat. "I think we should call Louise, have her come take a look at you."

"I don't think a doctor's going to help, or a priest either. I can't believe I'm saying this, but I think it's like Janna. When we close the case, it'll be done."

She shifted to him. "She cut me a little with her nails, see?" She held up her hand, palm out. "Said all this stuff about blood to blood and heart to heart. I had her blood all over me by then. And she said it wouldn't be finished until the promise was kept. And the thing is, I promised to find Beata while I was trying to keep the old woman alive."

"You made a blood pact with a Romany."

"A Romany speaker for the dead, apparently. Not on purpose," she added with some heat.

"An accidental blood pact," he qualified.

"You'd have done the same damn thing." Peeved, she shifted away again. "And you're a civilian. I'm a cop. Protect and serve, goddamn it."

"Which rarely includes blood pacts with dead travelers."

"Are you trying to piss me off?"

"Got your color back," he said easily.

"Well, whoopee. Eyes on the prize. I have to find out who killed Gizi Szabo, and I have to find Beata."

"She's alive, Beata. You're certain."

"In my current condition, tossing out the logic that says otherwise? I think Szabo would have known if the girl was dead. And I think I'd know it now. Instead, I have this certainty, against all that logic, that she's alive, trapped by the same devil who killed her great-grandmother. He wants to keep the girl, and the old woman made sure people knew she was getting close to finding her. Maybe she did that to lure him out, maybe she did it because it kept her going. But she was a threat."

Her nerves throttled down a few more notches when Roarke drove through the gates, when she saw the house. Home. Hers.

"Beata's a liability now," Eve added. "And that may weigh heavier on him than his need to keep her. Szabo stirred things up, and now I've done the same. He may decide to kill her rather than risk discovery."

"This Alexi Barin?"

"He's heading the list. He knew her, wanted her, got shut down by her. He's got an ego the size of Utah. He knew where she lived, where she worked, very likely knew her basic routine. Added, they were rehearsing for this big dance — *Diabolique*, Angel and Devil, which is no fucking coincidence."

"I'd agree. That would make it easier yet to lure her. Extra practice, after hours."

"There you go. He's had violent run-ins, got a sheet, and the cops who busted him all say he's got a temper that lights him up — quick and fast. And that's why he's not in Interview right now."

"Because while Szabo was killed violently and perhaps on impulse, if Beata's still alive, being held against her will, that took some planning. And continues to take planning."

"Right now, it's a good thing you can think like a cop, because I don't know if my brain's firing on all circuits." She got out of the car. "I need to be home. I need to be back in control. And if you're up for it, I could use some help running everybody on my list who knows Beata, studied with her, worked with her. Her neighbors, her friends, people who saw her routinely. You want what you see — or have to see it to want it."

"You give me the names, I'll start your runs — on the condition that you rest. An hour," he said as she started to protest. "Nonnegotiable."

"I just need to clear my head. And I'm starving," she admitted. "I feel like I haven't eaten in days, like everything's burned off."

"Possibly a side effect of possession."

"That's not funny either." She stepped inside, gave Summerset a beady stare. "*Baszd meg*," she suggested and watched his eyes widen.

Suspected she saw his lips twitch in what might have been a restrained smile.

"I see you're broadening your linguistics."

"That wasn't Russian," Roarke said as they headed up the stairs.

"I think it's Hungarian. It just came to me — and I figure he knows I just told him to fuck off."

"Rude, yet fascinating." He went with her to her office. "You, up." He pointed at the cat currently sprawled in Eve's sleep chair. "You, down," he ordered. "Give me your list, and I'll get those runs going." He brushed a hand over her hair, struggling against worry. "How about pizza?"

"I could eat a whole pie." She dropped into the chair. "Thank God my appetite's not running to that borscht, because I'd really rather have a brain tumor than beet soup." She dragged her notebook out of her pocket. "Most of the names are in here. I have to get more. Peabody and McNab were hitting the theaters where she worked or would have, and I need neighbors. But that's a big start."

"Food first." He walked into the kitchen.

Galahad didn't leap into her lap but sat eyeing her.

"I'm still me," she murmured. "I'm not her. I'm still me." When he bumped his head against her leg, her eyes stung. "I'm still me," she repeated.

Roarke came back with a plate on a tray. "I ordered up a whole one, but you start with that. And drink the soother. Don't argue," he warned. "I doubt you've looked in the mirror in the last few hours, but when I came in to the morgue, you looked like you belonged there. You'll eat, drink a soother, then we'll see."

With that, he turned to her desk, sat, and began inputting names into her computer. Eve ate like a horse.

"God, that's better. No shakes." She held out a hand, a steady one. "No queasiness, no jumps." Still she looked down at the cat. "He won't sit in my lap, even for pizza. He's not sure of me. I guess he senses something's off. That I'm off. How long do you think —" She couldn't say it.

"It's going to be fine." He rose to go to her. "We'll do whatever needs to be done, then we'll do whatever comes after that. You'll be fine."

"I have to live with the dead, Roarke, I don't want to chat with them. I see the advantage for a murder cop. Hey, sorry about the bad luck, but who killed you? Oh yeah, we'll go pick him up. Move on. I don't want to work that way. I don't want to live that way. I don't think I can."

"You won't have to." He took the tray, set it aside. "I swear to you, we'll find whatever needs finding."

She believed him. Maybe she had to, but she believed him.

"In the meantime . . ." She took his hand. "Can you be with me? I need to be *me*. I need you to touch me — me — and feel what I do when you're with me. Know that you feel me."

"There's no one but you." He slid onto the chair beside her. "Never anyone but you."

"Don't be gentle." She dragged his mouth to hers. "Want me."

She needed those seeking hands, that mouth hungry for hers. Needed to feel and taste and ache, needed to know that it was her mind, her body, her heart meshed with his.

Love, the dark and the light of it, was strength, and she took it from him.

He tugged her jacket down her shoulders, hit the release on her weapon harness as his mouth captured and conquered hers. And those hands, those wonderful hands lit fresh fires, a new fever that raged clean and bright in her blood. Her fingers fumbled for the chair controls so they tumbled back when it slid flat.

It wasn't comfort she wanted, he knew, but lust — the greed and speed. Perhaps he needed the same. So he pinned her arms over her head, used his free one to torment until she bucked beneath him, crying out as she came.

And there was more. Dewy flesh quivering under his hands, frantic pulses jumping at the nip of his teeth. The lust she wanted beat inside him as wildly as her heart.

208

His woman. Only his. Her flesh, her lips, her body. Strong again.

"Now. Yes. Now!" Her nails dug into his hips as she arched against him, opened to him.

Hot and wet, she closed around him, crying out again as he thrust hard and deep, as she bowed to take him. Holding there, holding for one heady moment as he looked in her eyes. As he saw only Eve.

Then the whirlwind, wicked and wild, spinning them both too high for air, too fast for fear.

And when the world settled back, all the colors and shapes and light, then came the comfort. She lay locked in his arms, breathing him in. Her body — her body — felt used and raw and wonderful.

Eyes closed, she ran a hand through his hair, down his back. "No problem, considering you might have just indirectly banged a ninety-six-year-old woman?"

"If I did, she gave as good as she got."

She laughed, tangled her legs with his. "We'll still bang when we're ninety, right?"

"Count on it. I'll have developed a taste for old women by then, so this could be considered good practice."

"It's got to be sick to even be thinking this way, but it's probably like making jokes in the morgue. It's how you get through." She untangled, sat up. "What I'm going to do is grab a shower, then coffee, then go over your runs. I'm going to work this like it needs to be worked and keep this other thing off to the side. Because if I think about it too hard, I'm just going to wig out."

He sat up with her, took her shoulders. And what she saw in his eyes blocked the air from her lungs. "What? What?"

"You are who you are. I know you. You believe that?"

"Yeah, but —"

"You're Eve Dallas. You're the love of my life. My heart and soul. You're a cop, mind and bone. You're a woman of strength and resilience. Stubborn, hardheaded, occasionally mean as a badger, and more generous than you'll admit."

Fear edged back, an icy blade down the spine. "Why are you saying this?"

"Because I don't think you can put what's happened aside, not altogether. Take a breath."

"Why —"

"Take a breath." he said it sharply, adding a shake so she did so automatically. "Now another." He kept one hand on her shoulder as he shifted and touched the other to her ankle.

And the tattoo of a peacock feather.

CHAPTER
EIGHT

She got her shower, got her coffee. She told herself she was calm — would be calm. Panic wouldn't help; raging might feel good, but in the end wouldn't help either.

"There are options," Roarke told her.

"Don't say the *E* word. No exorcisms. I'm not having some priest or witch doctor or voodoo guy dancing around me, banging on his magic coconuts."

"Magic . . . Is that a euphemism?"

"Maybe." It helped to see him smile — to think she might be able to. "But I'm not going there, Roarke."

"All right then. What about Mira?"

"You think she can shrink Szabo out of me?"

"Hypnosis might find some answers."

She shook her head. "I'm not being stubborn. Or maybe I am," she admitted when he cocked his eyebrows. "Right now I'd rather not bring anybody else into this. I just don't want to tell anybody I invited a dead woman to take up residence in my head, or wherever she is. Because that's what I did."

She shoved up, began to pace. "I said sure, come right in. Maybe if I'd been paying attention to what she was saying, what she meant, I'd have locked the door.

Instead I'm all, yeah, yeah, whatever, because I'm trying to keep a woman science says was already dead from bleeding out. It doesn't make any sense, goddamn it. And because it doesn't, I have to set it to one side. I have to," she insisted. "I have to work the cases — cases with my head, my gut. Fucking A mine. Which I damn well would've done anyway if she'd left me the hell alone."

"So you'll fight this with logic and instinct?" He decided they could both use a glass of wine.

"It's what I've got. It's what's mine. And if there's any logic to this other part, the part that makes no sense, when I find the killer, when I find Beata, it — she — goes away. If I don't believe that, I'm going to lock myself in a closet and start sucking my thumb."

He took her the wine, touched her cheek. "Then we'll find the killer and Beata. And for now, we'll keep the rest of it between you and me. Twenty-four hours. We'll work it your way, and I'll find someone who can undo what was done. If this isn't resolved in twenty-four hours, we'll work it my way."

"That sounds like an ultimatum."

"It most certainly is. You can waste time arguing, or you can get to work. I'm not going to share my wife with anyone for more than a day."

"I'm not your possession either, pal."

He smiled again. "But you belong to me. We can fight about it." He shrugged, sipped his wine. "And you'll have wasted part of your twenty-four. Still, it might fire you up, so I'm open to it."

"Smug bastard."

"Maybe you'd like to swear at me in Russian or Hungarian."

"And you said I was mean. Twenty-four." She took a slug of wine, considered how she's push for more if she needed it. "Let's look at the runs."

Roarke ordered data on-screen, leaned a hip against the side of her desk. "Your prime suspect," he began. "You had most of this, but the second-level run added a bit, and I extrapolated from your notes. Allie Madison's apartment, where it's verified Alexi Barin began the day, is an easy ten-minute walk to the alley — considerably less if a healthy, athletic man took it at a jog, even a run. It's about the same from the restaurant where he had brunch. As is his own apartment," Roarke added, ordering the map he'd generated on-screen. "These locations are clustered, more or less, in the general area."

"So he could've slipped out, slipped away, put on a mask, sliced Szabo up, and gotten back. Which would involve knowing she'd be in the alley at that convenient moment, and wearing something for the blood spatter. Because you don't hack somebody up the way she was hacked and walk away clean and fresh to take your alibi to brunch."

She paced in front of the screen. "He could have set a meet with her, pinning the timing. Told her he had some information on Beata. It's a lot of planning for an impulsive guy with a temper."

"Something set him off at the brunch if we go with your TOD, or prior if we stay with science," Roarke suggested. "He went to confront her, saw her in the alley — he'd have come from this direction, so he'd have passed the alley. He snaps, pulls the knife, goes in."

"Why is he disguised?"

"She could have seen his face, Eve. The condition she was in when you found her? It's not a stretch to believe she wasn't lucid."

"She didn't see it. She saw the devil." Eve paused a moment. "I know. It's what I saw. I had . . . a moment in the alley. I know what she saw."

"All right."

Because she'd expected an argument, even yearned for one, she rounded on him. "I don't know whether to be grateful or pissed off that you accept so easily."

"Not as easy as it might seem, just easier than you. So if you say you saw what she saw, I know you did. The occult, on some level, is involved — even that's logical."

"If you're a superstitious Irish guy."

"If you're currently able to curse in Hungarian and make goulash," he countered — and shut her up. "It could be your suspect has some power of his own."

"I'm not going there. Logic, facts, data. So while it's possible Alexi slipped out, did the murder, it's low on the logic and probability scale with the data we have at this time. Give me the guy Beata worked with. The one who walked out of the restaurant with her the night she was last seen."

"David Ingall, twenty-two, single. He's had two bumps. One for an airboard incident where he lost control and mowed down a group of pedestrians in

214

Times Square, and another for manufacturing and using false ID — he was underage and got into a sex club before an undercover busted him. He dropped out of NYU and takes a couple of virtual courses a semester, lives in a one-bedroom apartment a few blocks from the restaurant with two roommates. He's worked at Goulash for three years."

"Doesn't sound particularly murderous."

"In addition, the file from your Detective Lloyd has a statement from one of the roommates confirming his arrival home — and the drunken night of computer gaming that followed, on the night Beata Varga went missing."

"Roommates make it harder for him to take Beata, hold her, unless they're complicit."

"The information on the roommates is as benign as this one."

"Switch to the theater," Eve decided. "Where she was understudying. What did Peabody get?"

She studied the data as it scrolled, listened to Roarke's summaries. And paced.

None of them popped for her. Holding a woman against her will for an extended length of time required privacy, soundproofing, supplies, and time.

Maybe she was wrong — maybe the old woman had been wrong — and the girl was dead. And the thought of that pierced her so deep, she shuddered.

"Eve —"

"No, it's nothing. Keep going. I need to set up a murder board. I should've done it already."

She pinned up her photos, let the information Roarke provided wind through while she arranged what she needed on the board.

"Work and the school," Eve said. "Her most usual and regular spots other than her apartment. We focus there. She went out on auditions, and that'll be another level if we bomb here. Work, school, her neighbors. Then the theater, then audition sites, shops, and so on.

"Let me see the map again."

She moved closer to the screen. "She takes this route basically every day. Home to morning class. Then from class to work if she was scheduled. Back to class, back to work or an audition. Evening class three nights a week, and work again four nights."

"A regular customer at the restaurant," Roarke suggested. "Someone she waited on routinely. Wanted her, took her."

She nodded. "Possible. Someone she knew is most probable. Someone who could lure her where he wanted her to go. Doesn't make the ripples a forced abduction would. Had to have a place. Underground. A basement? A cellar?"

"The underground itself," Roarke commented. "There are places under the streets no one would pay attention to a woman struggling, screaming, calling for help."

"Too many," Eve agreed. "But it'd be risky. Someone could take her from you. Private," she said again. "Can you get the blueprints for the building — the dance school?" When his answer was simply a long look, she rolled her eyes. "Go ahead, show off. Let me see the uncle's data. Sasha Korchov."

"I've got deeper data on Natalya Barinova as well."

"It's a man. Go with the man first."

Benign. That was the word Roarke had used to describe Beata's coworker and his roommates. It was a word that came to mind with Sasha. Dreamy eyes, she remembered — a little like Dennis Mira there — and indeed his ID photo showed the same, along with the soft smile.

But the images Roarke had dug up from before the accident that had cost him his career and his lover showed a dynamic, intense, passionate man. Leaping, spinning a long, leanly muscled body showcased in dramatic costumes. The mane of hair coal black, the eyes on fire.

"How do you lose that?" she murmured. "Lose that energy, that passion, that fierceness? It must be almost like death or losing someone to death. Something breaks, something more than a leg, an arm. Something gets crushed, more than a foot, more than ribs."

How do you get over the anger — that's what she'd asked Lopez about survivors, about families who lost someone to murder.

"You lost your badge once," Roarke reminded her. "What did it do to you?"

"Destroyed me. Temporarily. Cut me off from what I was. But I had you to help bring me back, and I got my badge back. He lost his woman, too. His woman," she repeated. "Another dancer. And look here, they danced

217

the *Diabolique* ballet together. The Devil was his signature role. Son of a bitch. I should've seen it."

"The building has a basement," Roarke told her. "It runs the length and width of the building and holds a number of rooms, listed as storage and/or utility and maintenance on the plans."

"Who owns the building?"

"Funny you should ask. He owns it. He made quite a bit of money during his career and was awarded a large settlement after the accident."

"He's got no record anywhere. Unless it got covered up. No history of violence."

"Money can smooth the way."

"Yeah." She angled her head at Roarke. "It can. But you can usually find a few bumps in the media. Speculation, gossip. A man might not be charged and still be guilty."

"I'll see what I come across, and it's telling, I think, that he gave no interviews I can find, no public statements or appearances after the accident."

"He went underground," Eve murmured. "So to speak. Lost everything that mattered to him? That could be it. Had his sister, and she left her home and possibly the remains of her career to come here with him, bringing her infant son. Dreamy eyes," she recalled. "Medication? His medicals show extensive injuries from the accident, the kind a man's lucky to live through. Had to have a lot of pain."

More than physical, she decided, thinking of losing her badge again. Much more than physical pain.

"He sits in that studio now playing music for others to dance to. For this beautiful young woman who's about the same age, the same build and coloring as the woman he loved. She's going to dance that same role with his nephew."

"Would that piss him off, make him sad? They go to Vegas." She stopped as her gut twisted. "Natalya said they go to Las Vegas to be showgirls. Maybe Beata's not the first."

She strode to the auxiliary comp, started a search for missing persons, female of the same age group, coded in ballet.

"There's some speculation and juice regarding a young Sasha Korchov and his temper. Storming off stage at rehearsals, berating other dancers — neither of which is particularly unusual," Roarke added. "And more, here and there, about wild parties and breaking up hotel rooms and such. Before he met and danced with Arial Nurenski. She, it's speculated here, was balm to his troubled spirit and other romantic analogies. She changed him, calmed him, inspired him. They were to be married two weeks after the accident that killed her."

"Vanessa Warwich, age twenty-two, last seen leaving a café to go to rehearsal at the West Side School for the Arts. She was to dance the role of Angel in their autumn gala — just like Beata. That was two years ago. There are more." She looked over at Roarke. "I need to cross-reference, find a connection with the school or Barin, or the role."

"Send me your list. I'll take half."

She shot the data to his computer. "Roarke, if he's been taking these women, holding them, trapped in a basement? He is a devil."

They found eight.

CHAPTER
NINE

It was no backyard barbecue, but it had nearly the same guest list. In the conference room at Cop Central, Eve laid out what she had.

"Nine women over twenty-three years," she began, "with a direct or indirect connection to the school, or a connection to the ballet, have gone missing. All were in their early to mid twenties, dark hair, slim build. All were dancers, and all vanished without a solid explanation."

She turned to the screen, to the images. "In some cases they'd made some noises about leaving the city; in most there were personal items missing from their apartments, as if they had done so."

"The nine includes this Beata Varga." Commander Whitney studied the board Eve had arranged with ID shots of the missing. "Who connects to your murder victim."

"She's the latest. Detective Lloyd can give you the background on that." She nodded at him.

Lloyd stood and walked to the board. "Last seen leaving the restaurant where she worked. Here." He used the laser pointer Eve handed him. "In the company of two coworkers. They separated here, with

Beata continuing south in the direction of her apartment."

He went over the time lines, the other particulars, reviewed his interview statements. "Up to the point she went missing, she had regular contact with her family. Her work hours weren't regular, as her employers scheduled her around her classes and auditions and rehearsals, but when she was scheduled to work, she showed up, and statements from her employers, coworkers, customers corroborate she was responsible. Happy. Dedicated to forging her career. She'd just landed a part in an off-Broadway musical. She wasn't the type to just take off."

"Neither was Vanessa Warwich." Eve used her own pointer to highlight the photo. "Missing for twenty-six months, last seen leaving her apartment — here — to rehearse at the school. She'd enrolled only five weeks earlier, had a new boyfriend. Or Allegra Martin, age twenty-four, a principal dancer for the City Ballet who was starring in the role of Angel when she went missing four and a half years ago.

"Lucy Quinn, seven years missing," Eve continued, and worked down the line. "The pattern's clear, as is the victim type."

"You believe Sasha Korchov is replacing his lover with these women."

Eve nodded at Mira. "I know he is. He lost her, lost everything in one terrible moment. He left his home and is reduced to teaching others to dance, more to watching them — those young women — dance when his lover can't, while he plays for them."

"He plays the tune," Mira added. "They dance. If he's taken these women, it could be he needs them to dance for him — only him. He needs to keep them to himself, possibly to recreate the relationship he had with his fiancée, professionally and personally."

"Could they still be alive?" Peabody asked.

"I think there could only be one at a time," Mira told her. "One dancer, one lover, one partner if you will, or the illusion shatters. It would be more likely he's replacing the replacements over time than adding to the number."

"Beata's alive." Eve felt it in her bones. "But he's killed Szabo to protect himself. She made it known she believed Beata was alive and close by, trapped. Underground. A Romany, a dead talker, breathing down his neck."

She saw Baxter roll his eyes at that, stuck with logic. "He has some Romany blood. His sister and the old woman talked regularly — she's poking around, getting too close. He's afraid of her, superstitious. Enough so he disguises himself before he kills her. He doesn't want her to see his true face. And now he's had the cops at his door over it. How long can he keep Beata alive?"

"The pressure may push him to eliminate her," Mira agreed.

"I need a warrant. We need to search that basement, his apartment, the whole damn place."

"I can get one." APA Reo pushed to her feet. "The pattern and connections should be enough." She checked her wrist unit, winced at the time. "Waking up a judge or interrupting the Saturday night party isn't going to win me a popularity award."

As Reo left the room, Eve ordered the blueprints on-screen. "His apartment. We need to take him first, secure him so he doesn't have the chance to panic and take Beata out. We also secure the sister and nephew. They may be involved, may be protecting him. Feeney, I want to locate everyone in the building before we go in."

"We'll set it up. Get you heat source imagery."

"I need the exits secured," she continued. "And there are a lot of them: doors, windows, fire escapes, roof access. Elevators are down. If Korchov's in his apartment, we secure him. If he's not, we find him. We're also looking for the murder weapon. A dagger, seven and a quarter inches, likely a chipped tip. Renicki, Jacobson, you're on the apartment. Baxter, Trueheart, Peabody, we'll take the basement." She glanced at Roarke. "We'll take the civilian."

A locked door, she thought, would be easier to deal with if they had a thief — former — along.

"Feeney, McNab, Callendar, you run the electronics. I want locations, movements. Once the suspect, the sister, the nephew are secured, you'll move in."

She went over the rest of the assignments, detailing the operation stage by stage.

This is what she did, she told herself. This was the logic, the instinct, the training. And if there was something inside her urging her, all but begging her to hurry, she had to ignore it.

"I want all of you to watch your asses," she concluded. "This man is suspected of abducting and imprisoning at least nine women, very likely killing them when he was finished. He's suspected of slicing up a ninety-six-year-old woman in broad daylight. Just because he used to wear tights and ballet shoes doesn't mean he's not dangerous."

"Potentially very," Mira confirmed, "when cornered, when desperate. I'll ride with EDD," she added. "If any of his victims are alive, I may be able to help."

"Appreciate it." She looked at Morris. "And if they aren't."

He nodded. "Yes."

"Let's get moving. Load it up, ride it out. Father Lopez, if I could have a moment."

She gestured him to the side of the room. "I don't make a habit of calling a priest into an op, but —"

"I'm grateful you did in this case. I'll do whatever I can to help."

"You were there when Szabo died. You did the Last Rites thing. I figured if the old woman was Catholic, the girl probably is. Between you and Mira she'd be covered."

"It's kind of you."

She didn't know if it was — didn't know if it had been her impulse to call him in or if she'd been directed.

"How are you, Eve?"

"Hell if I know, and I don't have a lot of time to think about it right now."

"If you need me —"

"I'm hoping not to go there. No offense."

He smiled at her. "None taken."

"I'll need you to stay in the EDD van with Mira until we're clear."

"Understood, even if it's disappointing not to be able to get in on some of the action."

"This devil's my fight. Stick with Mira," she said before she started toward Roarke.

"I can't figure out how you connected the dots." Peabody stopped her. "The basement, all those missing women, the soft-spoken piano player. I feel like I missed a couple dozen steps."

"Things just started falling into place. Let's just say I followed Szabo. She was already closing in. Check with Reo. See if she's got the warrant."

She continued on to Roarke. "I need to ask you for something."

"Are you asking your husband or your civilian?"

"Looks like you're both. I need you to stay close to me. If I start to lose it —"

"You won't."

"If, I think you can help me stay grounded. She's in here." Eve touched a hand to her chest. "This is the guy who took Beata, the guy who killed her. She might want some payback. If it looks like I'd turn that way, stop me. You stop me."

"I have every confidence in Lieutenant Dallas, but if it makes you feel easier, I won't let you do anything you'll regret."

"Good. But be, you know, subtle about it."

He had to laugh. "You are absolutely you. All right then, while preventing you from taking a dead Gypsy's

226

revenge, I'll do whatever I can to preserve your dignity. How's that?"

"It'll do."

She reviewed the blueprints again on the way to the building, checked in with her teams, focused on the work.

"We go in the front, pass the main stairs, to the right and straight to the basement access door. It's going to be locked. If the master doesn't work, we use the battering ram or" — she glanced at Roarke — "other means. If Feeney picks up images down there, we follow his lead. Otherwise, Peabody, Baxter, Trueheart, take this sector. Roarke and I this one. One of you sees a mouse riveting, everybody hears about it. We clear sector by sector. If a door's locked, take it down. Call for backup if you need it."

She toggled to the exterior view. "Locations of cams are highlighted. I don't see anybody watching them this time of night. But there are very likely cams down there not on the blueprints."

Think like him, she ordered herself. Not like a frantic old woman.

"He'd want to watch her, and want his area secured in and out. Can't have somebody stumbling across her, and can't let her find a way out. If Renicki and Jacobson lock him down, they can work him for more information — but we won't count on getting it. We'll bring in the others, and we'll go through every inch of that basement.

"Feeney," she said into her mic, "give me the word."

"Got nothing in the suspect's place. Got two in the other apartment. Everything else aboveground is clear. Got nothing for you in the basement, but there are voids down there, Dallas, either due to the thickness of walls, jammers, or sensor blocks."

"Tucks them up tight," she murmured. "Give me the location of the voids."

She keyed them in, felt the adrenaline begin to pump. "We hit those first. If he's not upstairs and didn't go for a goddamn walk, he's down there with her now. We're green. All teams, we're green. Move."

She jumped out of the back of the transport, weapon out. She prayed she hadn't missed a deeper level of security, prayed he wasn't monitoring the cameras as she used her master to access the main door.

Cops spread out to the exits, up the stairs, moving quick and quiet while she and her team rushed to the basement door.

"Master's ineffective."

"Give me a minute," Roarke told her. "Battering rams are crude, and they're noisy."

She stepped back to give him room, mentally checking off each exit as her men reported them secure.

When Roarke's clever tools and fingers unlocked the door, she signaled to Peabody. "High and left," she told her, "then straight down."

She went in low and right — and knew immediately her instincts had been on target.

Lights burned in the ceiling, dim but activated. The old metal stairs led down to a concrete floor, thick walls, narrow corridors.

228

She signaled Peabody to lead her team, then set off in the opposite direction with Roarke.

They passed through a cavernous room piled with old furniture, lamps, fabrics, down another dim corridor. She heard the clink and hum of the building mechanicals as they moved through a utility area where tools were neatly stored on freestanding shelves.

"This area needs to be maintained," she said quietly, sweeping with her weapon as Roarke did the same with the one he'd slipped out of his pocket. "Wherever he keeps them has to be soundproofed and fully secured."

"This sector's void's west. Down that way."

Eve started to turn, then went into a crouch, weapon up. Her muscles trembled as the ballerina blocked her way.

"I can't get out," the woman said and held out her hands. "We can't get out. Can you help me?"

"You have to wait."

"Eve?"

"It's Vanessa Warwich." Eve fought off shudders as her skin shivered from the sudden cold. "You have to wait a little longer."

"I couldn't dance anymore." She lifted her sparkling white skirt. "He cried when he killed me." She touched her fingers to the gaping slice across her throat. "But I couldn't dance anymore."

"Just wait." And gritting her teeth, Eve walked through the pleading woman. She reached out to try to balance herself when her head spun.

Roarke grabbed her, braced her. "Bloody hell. Stay here."

"I have to finish it. You know I have to finish it. I have to make it stop." She glanced back and into Vanessa Warwich's eyes but saw the others behind her. All the pretty girls in their sparkling skirts and toe shoes.

All those white throats gaping.

"She's waiting. Warwich waiting — trapped. And God, she's not alone. We have to move."

"Hold on to me if you have to."

He took the lead, brooked no argument. She steadied herself as she followed, cleared her throat as she listened to team updates.

Her op, she reminded herself. She was in command here. She had to be.

Natalya and Alexi were secured, Peabody had reached the first of her voids. An empty room. The search of Sasha's apartment was under way, but neither he nor the murder weapon had been found.

Roarke held up a hand, stopped her. "Sensors," he murmured. "They'll read us."

"Then we're getting close."

"They'll likely signal in his apartment but could very well alert him if he's down here. Give me a minute to jam them."

"You're handy."

"We do what we can." He took out what looked like an innocent PPC, keyed in various codes. "It's rudimentary," he told her. "Just a precaution to let him know if anyone's down this way."

"Or if his current ballerina managed to get out. Are we clear?"

"We are."

"Peabody, we hit sensors. Watch for them. We're moving."

Another turn, another twenty feet, and they spotted the door. "Secured door," she said into her mic. "Accessing now."

She rolled her shoulders as Roarke got to work. She was ready, she thought. She was herself.

When he nodded, they went through the door together, swept it.

She supposed it would be called a sitting room — windowless, but with a softly faded carpet, a sofa, a lamp. And a small monitoring station.

He could sit here and watch her before he went in, she thought, studying the blank monitor, then the second secured door, the one painted bright bloodred.

"The red door," she murmured. "Locked behind the red door."

Without a word Roarke went to the door, checked the security. She had to breathe deeply, slowly, fighting the voice inside her begging her to hurry, hurry, hurry.

"Got his lair," she said to Peabody. "Key in on me. Secondary door and inner security being bypassed. Feeney, I've got a monitoring station here. Send McNab in. We're clear," she said at Roarke's nod. "We're going in."

She looked at him, trusted him to keep her centered. She held up three fingers, closed to a fist, then held up one, two. On three they were through the door.

CHAPTER
TEN

He'd set his prison with a stage with filmy white curtains on either side and lights to enhance the mood of the music that soared. Roses, their petals glowing silver in the light, scented the air. Eve spotted all this, and another door, in an instant, but her focus centered on the stage and the dancers.

Beata, her face pale with exhaustion, her eyes empty of hope, wore a white, filmy skirt, topped by a bodice glittering with gold like the ring that crowned her.

The same costume as all the others. All the pretty dancers.

Beata rose, fluid as water, *en pointe* and into an arabesque before turning into the arms of the devil.

He gripped her waist, lifted her high, while his eyes shone through the holes in his mask. His cape flowed from his shoulders as he dipped her head toward the floor.

Eve's weapon seemed to burn in her hand. She longed to fire it, craved it as her heart raged in her chest. And the words, the thoughts that roared through her head were in Romany.

Roarke touched a hand to the small of her back, just a bare brush of fingers. "Your move, Lieutenant," he murmured beneath the swell of music.

Her move, she thought, and took it when the dancers leaped apart.

"Nice jump," she called out, training her weapon on Sasha. "Now freeze, or I'll drop you off your twinkle toes."

She heard Beata's cry, swore she felt it rip through her soul, but kept her eyes on Sasha.

"You're interrupting the performance." He spoke with some heat — as a man would when bumped violently on the street by a stranger.

"Show's canceled."

"Don't be ridiculous." He dismissed her with a wave of the hand, then reached it out for his partner. Roarke had already moved in and put himself between them.

Sasha pulled the dagger from his belt. "I'll kill you for touching her."

"You can certainly try, and I admit I'd enjoy beating you to hell and back again, but I believe the lieutenant will indeed drop you if you take a step toward this girl."

"She's mine." He whirled back to Eve. "No one takes her from me. She is my Angel, and here she lives forever."

"I am Beata Varga." Beata yanked the crown from her head, heaved it. "I'm not your Angel, and you go to hell."

Sasha lunged for her, and even as Roarke braced to counter the attack, Eve kept her word. She dropped him, stunned and shuddering, to center stage.

As he fell, Beata covered her face with her hands and slid to the floor at the edge of those glittering lights. "I knew someone would come. I knew someone would come."

Eve moved forward, went to her knees, and wrapped her arms around Beata as Peabody's team rushed in.

Once again Roarke stepped between. "I think you might want to restrain your suspect before he recovers, and take him out. Give Beata a moment." He gave the dagger a light kick across the stage. "And there's your murder weapon."

"Yeah." If Peabody thought it strange to see her partner rocking the weeping girl, she said nothing of it. "We'll clear him out, and I'll tell Father Lopez and Dr. Mira to stand by."

"Crazy fucker." Baxter looked around the room as he locked restraints on Sasha. "All his world's a freaking stage. Trueheart tagged the MTs. For her," he added, and with Trueheart's help, hauled Sasha to his feet.

Eve let the police routine play out behind her — under control, she thought and concentrated on Beata. "Are you hurt? Did he hurt you?"

"Not really, not much. How long? How long have I been here? Sometimes he gave me something that made me sleep, and I lost track."

"You're all right now. That's what counts."

"He locked me in. In there." Though she continued to shake, she lifted her chin toward the inner door. "This horrible, beautiful room. He brought me flowers and chocolates, and all these beautiful clothes. He's out of his mind, out of his mind." She dropped her head back on Eve's shoulder.

"Did he touch you? Beata." She drew the girl back.

"No, no, no. Not that way. I thought he would rape me, kill me, but it wasn't what he wanted."

She continued to tremble under Eve's hands, but even as they streamed with tears, her eyes held fury.

"He said we would be together forever, and I would do what I was born to do: dance. Always dance. And night after night he would come and put on the costume. If I wouldn't wear mine, he'd give me the drug, and when I woke I'd be in it. So I put it on rather than have him touch me. And I danced, because if I refused or if I fought, he'd tie me and leave me in the dark."

"You did what you had to do," Eve told her. "You did exactly right."

"I called, but no one heard, and I tried to break the door, but I couldn't. I couldn't. I couldn't."

"Okay. It's okay."

"Every day I'd try to find a way out, but there wasn't one. I don't know where I am. How did you find me?"

"You're in the basement of the school where you took classes. We'll get into all the details later. We're going to get you out of here now."

"My family."

"You can contact them." Eve laid a hand on Beata's cheek. "Your family is always with you, wherever you are, wherever you go."

Beata closed a hand around Eve's wrist, let her head rest in Eve's hand. "That's what my grandmother would say to me whenever I was sad or scared."

I know, Eve thought, and helped Beata to her feet. "I want you to go with these officers now. They'll take you out."

"Aren't you coming with me?"

"I'll be there soon. There are things I have to do. Beata, did they know, were they part of this? Natalya, Alexi."

"No. He said it was only us, our secret — that they wanted him to be calm, to accept, to live without me. Her, Arial, the one whose name he called me. But that he never would. He wouldn't share me with them or the world. He wouldn't lose me this time. He told me often."

"Okay, go ahead now. Go outside. Go breathe the air."

Eve knew what it was to be locked up, to be trapped and helpless. And to want to breathe free.

Eve shut off her recorder, looked at Roarke. "It's not done. I hoped, when we found her . . . I have to find the others. I know where they are," she said before Roarke answered. "They're pressing on me. The dead. I know where they are, and I think — hope — I know what to do."

"Then we'll go find them."

She turned her recorder back on, reengaged her mic. "I need a unit down here with tools. We need to take down a wall. And I'll need Morris. I'm on the move. Key in on my location when I get there, and send a team down to process this goddamn prison.

"Let's go," she said to Roarke.

She didn't have to ask him to hold her hand, to keep her close as they walked those dim corridors, or to talk to her quietly, soothingly.

"He must've built that place years ago," she said. "And updated it, maintained it — down here in the bowels of the building. There were tools in that utility room we went through. A sledgehammer and —"

"I'll get something." She was pale again, he thought, feverish again. It had to end. "Are you all right alone?"

"I'm not exactly alone, but yeah."

While Roarke doubled back, she walked straight to the void, the empty room Peabody had reported, stared — her eyes burning dry — at the far wall. Old wood, old brick, so it looked patched and repaired and nondescript. But she felt the misery, the horror, and had to force herself not to attack it with her bare hands.

Morris came in behind her. "I passed Roarke. He told me to bring this."

She grabbed the pry bar out of his hands, began to drag at the boards, the spikes and nails.

"Dallas —"

"They're back there. Trapped in there."

"Who?"

"The others. All the others. They can't get out, can't get to the other side. They need to be seen, need to be shown." Her muscles trembled with the effort as boards splintered. "They need help."

"Step back," Roarke snapped as he strode in. "Eve, step back."

He slammed the sledgehammer he carried at the brick, exploding dust and shards. As he pounded again,

again, she moved in, away from the arc of his swing to rip and pry.

The stench seeped in, one she knew too well. Death entered the room.

"I see her." Eve grabbed for the flashlight on her belt. "Her — them. Three, I think. Wrapped in plastic."

As she spoke, Roarke slammed the hammer again. Through the gap he created a skeletal hand reached out, palm up, as if in supplication.

"Careful now." Morris laid a hand on Eve's shoulder. "We need to go carefully now. This is for my team and forensics."

"Let me see your light." Roarke took it from Eve, shone it in the gap. "Christ Jesus. He's stacked them, like berths in a bloody train."

"And when bricks were too much trouble or he just ran out of them, he switched to boards. Can you see how many?" Eve asked him.

"Five, I think. I can't be sure."

"Hold off now. It's enough." She took out her communicator. "Peabody, we've got bodies. Eight, maybe more. I need a recovery team, the sweepers. Morris is calling his people in."

"Acknowledged. Jesus, Dallas, eight?"

"Maybe more. They're found now. And Peabody, send down the priest."

She clicked off, said nothing as Roarke picked up the bar and continued to carefully knock away loose bricks. Instead she reached in, laid a hand on the plastic covering the ruined shell of Vanessa Warwich.

You're found now, she thought. You're free now.

She stepped out of the room, just leaned against a wall as she struggled against waves of grief.

And the old woman stepped to her, spoke.

"You found our Beata."

"I'd have found her my own way. I'd have stopped this my own way."

"I think perhaps you would. But the child is so precious to me, how could I risk it? I was guided to you, or you to me, when I was between. Who can say?"

"I'd think you could at this point. Death ought to come with a few answers."

Now Gizi smiled. "Perhaps it will. You didn't kill him."

"It's not how I work."

"I would have," she said simply, "but your way will be enough. You are the warrior. I can leave the gift with you."

"No. Seriously."

"Then it goes with me. I had a good, long life, but he didn't have the right to end it. You'll see there is balance."

"He'll pay, for all of it." She hesitated, then asked what she had asked Lopez, asked herself. "Is it enough?"

"This time. For others?" Gizi lifted her shoulders, let them fall. "Who can say?"

"This time then. I have to finish. I have to finish my way."

"Yes. As do I. You've freed them. Now I'll guide them to the other side where there will be light and peace. Until we're called again. *Pa chiv tuka*, Eve Dallas."

"*Ni eve tuka.*" Eve shook her head. "You're welcome," she corrected.

She saw the light again, not blinding now, but warm. She simply closed her eyes as the heat flowed through her, then out again. When she opened them, there was nothing but the dim corridor and the sound of approaching footsteps.

She pushed away from the wall, moved forward to direct cops and techs. To do her job. "They're in there," she said to Lopez. "Maybe you can do . . . what you do."

"Yes. The girl, Beata, she's waiting for you. She won't leave until she speaks to you."

"I'll go up."

"A very hard day," he said. "And yet . . ."

"Yeah." She reached over as Roarke came out, brushed mortar and brick dust off his shirt. "Let's go up."

"Tell me how you are."

"I'll show you." She stopped, yanked up her pants leg. Her clutch piece rode on her unmarked ankle. "No more tattoo. It's a lot less crowded in here." She tapped her head. "Say something in Russian."

"I only have a few phrases, but this one seems appropriate. *Ya liubliu tebia.*"

She grinned at him, felt a lightness she hadn't felt in hours. "I have no idea what you said. Thank God."

He grabbed her, held tight. Then he drew her face up, crushed his mouth with hers.

"On an op," she murmured but kissed him back before drawing away.

Linking hands, they continued down the corridor. "I said I love you — and it's true in every language."

"Nice. Let's just keep it all in English for a while. God, I'm starving again." She pressed her hand to her belly. "Anyway, thanks for the assist. In there and all around."

"No problem. But next time we have a barbecue, Lieutenant, we both stay the bloody hell home."

"That's a deal."

Upstairs she paused, walked over to where Natalya and Alexi sat on the steps, nodded at the cop standing by them. Natalya looked up, eyes flooded with tears.

"They said — we heard — there are bodies."

"Yes."

"My brother." Her voice broke as she pressed her face to her son's chest. "He was broken, but he took his medication. We went on — we both went on. What has he done? In the mercy of God, what has he done?"

"She didn't know." Alexi held her close while she sobbed. "We didn't know, I swear it. My uncle, he's such a quiet man. Such a quiet man. Beata? She's all right?"

"She'll be all right. We're going to have to take you and your mother down to Central. We need to talk."

He only nodded and stroked his mother's hair. "We didn't know."

"I believe you."

"A nightmare for them," Roarke commented as they stepped outside into the warm night.

"One that won't end anytime soon."

Gawkers pressed behind the barricades. Cops swarmed, lights flared, and the air was busy with voices and communicators. Reporters, alerted to the scene, shouted questions.

Eve ignored them all as Beata broke away from Mira and ran to her.

"They said Mamoka is dead. Sasha killed her — my great-grandmother."

"Yes. I'm very sorry."

The sound she made was deep, dark grief. "Mamoka. She came for me, to find me. And he killed her."

"He'll pay for that, for all of it." And this time, Eve reminded herself, it was enough. "She did find you, and that's what mattered most to her. She told me your name. She . . . showed me the way."

"She spoke to you?"

"She did. And I know she's okay, because you are. You can see her tomorrow. I'll arrange it. But now, you need to go to the health center, get checked out. You need to listen to Dr. Mira. We'll talk again."

"There were others." Her face stark, Beata stared at the old building with its glittering windows. "I heard —"

"We'll talk again," Eve said.

Beata pressed her fingers to her eyes, nodded, then dropped them. "I'm sorry. I never asked your name."

"I'm Dallas." Through and through, she thought, in and out and all the way. "Lieutenant Eve Dallas."

"Thank you, Lieutenant Dallas." Beata held out a hand. "For every day of the rest of my life."

"Make good use of them." Eve shook her hand, then sent her back to Mira.

Eve took a breath, then tuned in to the lights, the noise, the movement. Her world, she thought, and walked back to Roarke.

"Things to wrap up," she told him. "Reports to file, killers to question."

"You look pretty pleased about it."

"All in all, I am. But tomorrow? Why don't we stay home, watch old vids and eat junk food, maybe drink a whole bunch of wine and have half-drunk sex?"

"A master plan. I'm in."

"Excellent. I have to go back down there. You could wait here or go on home."

"Lieutenant." He took her hand again. "I'm with you."

"Well, you're handy," she said, grinned again.

She walked back toward the building with him to do the job. She felt tired, violently hungry, and completely herself.